POP. SPLAT.

"And you're a professional?" asked Remo.

"Right. Here's why."

One moment, Wetherby was standing, talking. The next moment, he was in the air, heading toward Remo. His right leg was cocked underneath his flying body. Remo recognized the move. The right leg would come into the top of his body. As Remo fell backward Wetherby would land, and the next step would be a killing hand-blow to Remo's temple—if it was done right.

To be done right, it could not be done to Remo.

Wetherby's leg lashed out. The foot took Remo heavily in the right shoulder. Remo did not go down. He struck back. He stepped backward one step, saw Wetherby's midsection as open as a church basket, and put his own foot into the policeman's solar plexus.

It was over that fast. Wetherby's blow. Pop. Remo's response. Splat.

Wetherby dropped to the floor. His eyes stayed open.

"Crap," said Remo. "Crap and double crap." Another suicide pilot dead in an attack, and Remo still had no information . . .

The Destroyer Series

The Destroyer

ASSASSINS PLAY-OFF #20

by Richard Sapir & Warren Murphy

PINNACLE BOOKS • NEW YORK CITY

This is a work of fiction. All the characters and events portrayed in this book are fictional, and any resemblance to real people or incidents is purely coincidental.

THE DESTROYER: ASSASSINS PLAY-OFF

An original Pinnacle Books edition, published for the first time anywhere.

ISBN: 0-523-00708-6

First printing, September 1975

Cover illustration by Hector Garrido

Printed in the United States of America

PINNACLE BOOKS, INC.
275 Madison Avenue
New York, N.Y. 10016

ASSASSINS PLAY-OFF

He who plays with the sword shall succumb to him who works with the willow branch.

—HOUSE OF SINANJU.

CHAPTER ONE

He had paid $8,000, all that was in his family's savings account, and had promised $12,000 more in three years of monthly installments to be sitting in the drafty main room of this Scottish castle in the drizzly, bitter chill autumn of the highlands, his knuckles on the floor, his weight on his knees in a position of respect.

They had remodeled the room, they said. A new wooden floor, polished to a high gloss. New rice-paper tapestries with the symbols of Ninja—the night fighters—of Atemi, the fist methods; of Kung Sool, the archery; of Hsing-i, the boxing; and many others he did not recognize.

But they had not taken away the draft from Kildonan Castle, north of Dundee and south of Aberdeen, inland from the Firth of Tay. Only the Scots, thought William Ashley, could create a structure that was drafty without being ventilated.

And even the Koreans couldn't overcome it.

The large room smelled of pungent sweat mixed with fear and perhaps it was the chill that made Ashley's knees ache and his back feel as if someone were tightening a garrote on his spinal column. Not since he was a novice in the little commercial karate dojo in Rye, New York, had Ashley felt the pain in the position of respect, knees on floor, hands extended outward so that you rested on both feet and hands. It was in that little dojo after work that he learned respect for himself in the conquest of his body. Learned to control his fears and his passions, learned that it was not the yellow belt or the green belt or the brown belt or even the highest—or what he thought was the highest then—the black belt, that was important; no, what was important was what he became with each step taken toward a perfection far off in the distance.

And it was precisely this striving for perfection that had brought Ashley to the highlands with his family's savings and his three-week annual vacation.

He had initially thought that perfection was an unattainable goal, a thought that kept men rising and improving, a goal that when you were closest you realized was farther away. A place and a thing beyond where you would ever be. It was a direction, rather than a destination.

Which is what he had said in the Felt Forum of Madison Square Garden last month. Which was why he was here, $8,000 poorer and telling himself, like all those who really understand the martial arts, that body pain must eventually diminish.

He had made the remark about perfection being unattainable to a Korean who had come to the annual martial arts exhibit and who had commented somewhat complimentarily on Ashley's performance.

"Almost perfect," said the Korean, who wore a dark business suit with white starched shirt and a red tie. He was young but somewhat fleshy around the jowls.

"Then I am happy," said Ashley, "because no one is perfect."

"Not so," said the Korean. "There is perfection."

"In the mind," said Ashley.

"No. Here on earth. Perfection you can touch."

"What school are you with?" asked Ashley, who himself was karate but knew of kung fu, aikido, ninja, and many other fighting methods of the body.

"Perhaps all schools," said the Korean. Ashley looked at the man more closely. He could not be older than his thirties, and such arrogance in one so young surely meant ignorance rather than competence. He reminded himself that not all Orientals knew the martial arts any more than all Americans knew rocketry. The man had obviously come to the Felt Forum to see what the martial arts were about and just as obviously was a windbag. There were Orientals who talked through their hat, too.

The Korean smiled.

"You doubt me, don't you, William Ashley?" he said.

"How do you know my name?"

"Do you think your name is a secret?"

"No, but I am surprised that you know me."

"William Ashley, thirty-eight, computer programmer for Folcroft Sanitarium, Rye, New York. And you think because you are a grain of sand on the beach, I should not be able to tell you from any other grain of sand on the beach, and you are surprised that I know you."

"Very," said Ashley who knew what to do in situations like this. He was supposed to call Folcroft Sanitarium and report it because the information he worked with at the sanitarium was top security. The sanitarium walls were just a cover. He, along with two other National Security Agency programmers, had

3

been sent there seven years before, and so secret was their work that no one man could tell, even if he were forced to, about the scope and nature of any project he worked on.

But something about this Korean made Ashley hesitate.

"If you are surprised, you have a very poor memory."

Bill Ashley slapped his thigh and laughed.

"Of course. I remember. Last year. Just before Christmas. You had been in some sort of accident, with crude oil, I think, and had suffered skin burn. Severe, if I remember. You came to our dojo and you were recuperating and our sensei said you were a great master. Your name was, don't tell me, I remember, I remember, I remember . . ."

"Winch."

"Right. Winch," said Ashley. "How do you do, sir. It is an honor to meet you again. Oh, I'm sorry." Ashley put his hand down. He remembered the man did not shake hands.

Together then, they watched an exhibition of monkey fighting, a peculiar form in which much leverage was claimed, but Winch pointed out to Ashley that there was no leverage at all, just the illusion of power.

When one of the fighters knocked the other off the mat, Ashley said that looked like plenty of leverage to him.

"Only because they were both monkey style, balancing on a single foot, instead of thrusting from that foot. Anyone with feet wide apart who got close so that he could see the little lines on the teeth could,

4

with a push, make any monkey fighter look like a fool."

"I believe it because you say it, but they are both fifth dan black belts."

"You do not believe it, but you will," Winch said and rose from his seat. In a language Ashley assumed was Korean, Winch spoke to several of the monkey fighting masters who looked shocked, then angry.

"Put on your gi," said Winch. "You will make the monkey boxer look like a fool."

"But they are all very famous here in the New York area," said Ashley.

"I have no doubt. Many people are famous here. Just keep your feet wide apart and get very close and push."

"Perhaps a more forceful attack?" said Ashley.

"A push," said Winch.

"What did you tell them?" asked Ashley, nodding past Winch toward the black belt experts who were staring at him.

"What I told you. That you will make any monkey boxer look like a fool and that they should be ashamed that true Koreans would lend their presence to such silliness."

"Oh, no. You didn't," gasped Ashley.

"Go," said Winch.

"What about humility?"

"What about truth? Go. You will shame that monkey boxer if you do as I say. Do not box. Do not attack with feet or slashing or chopping blows. Get close and push. You will see."

When Ashley, in his two piece gi, entered the ring, he heard snickers from the black belts. He saw several

5

smile. The monkey boxer chosen to take care of Ashley smiled. He was about the same age as Ashley, but his body and even his skin was harder, more alive, for he had been training since he was a child. Ashley had started when he was twenty-eight.

Ashley bowed his respect before the match, but the monkey boxer, apparently angered by Winch's derision, stood rocklike, unmoving, ungiving of respect. A low murmur went through the crowd around the ring. This was not to be done. This was twice that tradition had been broken. First with the open insult from Winch, and then with the monkey boxer's failure to honor his opponent.

It was then that Ashley, looking at his opponent's face, knew the man meant to kill him. It was a smell as much as anything, his own body emitting something that told him he held his own life in his hands and he did not want it there.

Ashley desperately wanted to assume some known form of defensive position he had learned, but a greater force took over. His mind. He knew he should not be on the mat with this expert in the first place. Nothing he had ever learned would be good enough to compete with this man staring hate from his brown slanted eyes, the face twisted, the teeth bared, the body rising on the tips of the toes, and then one foot leaving for the spring. Only something Ashley had never tried before might work. He was committed to what Winch had told him.

The lights were hot overhead and the crowd seemed to disappear as he forced his unwilling body to approach the master, as he forced his feet wide for a solid stance—and then, as he saw the flash of the monkey boxer striking at his eyes, he also saw the tiny lines of ridge on the man's teeth, and Bill Ashley pushed forward, his hand coming to the boxer's chest.

Later he would tell people he did not know what happened. But there, in the heat of the center of the mat, he felt his hand go into the hard chest of the monkey boxer, and the boxer's blow forced his own body around Ashley's hand like the spoke of a wheel moving around the hub, and the monkey boxer hit the mat with a thwack. Ashley's hand was still out there in front of him. The boxer twitched and a drop of blood reddened the white mat under the dark black oriental hair.

"I just pushed. Not hard," said Ashley.

A few hands clapped and it became applause and a doctor ran up into the ring, and Ashley kept telling everyone he had just pushed. Really, that was all he had done.

He bowed to the ring, now full of desperate nervous men.

"He'll live," said the doctor. "He'll live."

"He'll live," announced the chairman of the event.

"It may just be a concussion," said the doctor. "Stretcher. Stretcher."

And that was how it had begun. Ashley had dinner with Winch and learned about a new concept in perfection, frightening in its simplicity.

William Ashley had, all his life, simply believed the opposite about what perfection was. He had believed it was something martial artists moved toward. But it was the other way around. Perfection was what they all came from.

As Mr. Winch explained, there was a method, a

way, that had to do with the way things moved and were, that was perfect execution of the art. There was one martial art at the beginning, in the deep, deep past of the Orient. From this one art came all the others with all their codes and all their disciplines. And, inasmuch as they differed from this sun source, they were less.

"Could I learn it?" asked Ashley. They were eating at Hime of Japan, a restaurant on the other side of Manhattan from Madison Square Garden that served a more than passable teriyaki. Ashley maneuvered his chopsticks with skill, creating little crevices with his rich brown meat and vegetables to catch the pungent sour sauce. Winch had only a spoonful of rice, which appeared to take forever for him to finish.

"No," said Winch, answering Ashley's question. "One cannot put the ocean into a brandy snifter."

"You mean I'm unworthy?"

"Why must you make a moral judgment? Is a brandy snifter unworthy of the ocean? Is it not good enough for the ocean? Is it too evil for the ocean? No. A brandy snifter is a brandy snifter and will take a brandy snifter full of salt water. If you must moralize, it is good enough for a brandy snifter of the ocean. But for no more."

"I have a confession to make," said Ashley. "When I saw the monkey boxer first strike canvas, I hoped he was dead. I kept saying that I only pushed, but I had this sort of fantasy, well, that I had killed him, and I honestly hoped I had killed him, and that it would make me famous."

Mr. Winch smiled and leaned back in his seat. He

8

placed his stubby yellow hands with the slightly long fingernails on the table.

"Let me tell you about perfection. All these forms that you have learned come from the killing forms. But they are not a game, as you and the others make of them. A man who makes a game of these things will succumb to a child who does things properly. You were right in your feelings, right to wish that the monkey boxer were dead, because that is what the sun source of the martial arts was designed to do. To kill."

"I want to learn perfection."

"What for? You don't need it."

"I want to learn it, Mr. Winch. I need it. I need to know it. If I have but one life and I do one thing in it, then I would know this perfection."

"You have not listened, but then you are a brandy snifter, and I know brandy snifters and what brandy snifters will do. So let me say now, the cost is high."

"I have savings."

"The cost is very high."

"How much?"

"High."

"In money?"

"In money," said Mr. Winch, "twenty thousand dollars. That is the money price."

"I can give you nine thousand now and pay off the rest."

"Give me eight thousand. There is some traveling to do."

"I can't go out of the country without clearance. It's sort of a job requirement."

"Oh. Are you in the CIA?"

"No, no. Something else."

"Well, then, brandy snifter, we'll have to forget it. Just as well, too. There is a very high price."

"Couldn't you teach me here?"

"That's not the point," said Mr. Winch. "The point is I am not doing it here. I teach at a place in Scotland."

"Out of the country. Damn. Still, it's this side of the Iron Curtain and maybe, just maybe, my people will think Scotland is secure."

"They will, brandy snifter, they will. English-speaking peoples have a well of trust that is bottomless. For other English-speaking peoples. I will see you at Kildonan Castle with your eight thousand dollars, brandy snifter."

Bill Ashley did not tell his wife about the $8,000, and he hid the savings book so that she would not find out. He did not know what he would say when he eventually told her. He would have to tell her, he knew, but he would take care of that after he had seized his share of perfection, as much as he could absorb.

The job was something else. While the National Security Agency only used Folcroft as a cover for the information bank Ashley worked on, he still had to get vacation permission from the director of the sanitarium, Dr. Harold W. Smith.

Ashley was always careful to maintain his cover precisely when talking to the crusty old New Englander who thought the information banks contained data on some sort of mental health survey. Ashley always read from the looseleaf notebook on what he

10

was allegedly supposed to be working on before he entered Dr. Smith's office.

One thing had always struck him as odd, though. Dr. Smith, who was not supposed to be that concerned with what his staff was specifically doing, had a computer terminal to the left of his desk, and unless the NSA had done some clever short-circuiting, that terminal appeared as if it could get a readout from every computer core in the sanitarium.

Ashley was sure however that NSA was not about to do some dumbass thing like let the cover know what it was covering. Still, it was disconcerting to see it there, disconcerting to just entertain the possibility that the director of a sanitarium might have access to highly classified secrets, information so sensitive that no single programmer had access to work outside of his own, and no two were allowed to socialize.

"So you wish to take a vacation?" said Smith. "Early, I see."

"A bit. I feel I could use it, sir."

"I see. And where are you and your wife going?"

"Well, I sort of thought I'd go alone this time. A real vacation. I need it."

"I see. Do you often take vacations alone?"

"Sometimes."

"Oh. When was your last vacation alone?"

"In 1962, sir."

"You were a bachelor then, weren't you?"

"Yes. If you must know, sir, I'm having trouble with my wife and I just want to get away from her. I've got to get away for a little while."

"Do you think your work will suffer if you don't?" asked Smith.

"Yes, sir."

"Well, I see no reason why you shouldn't get a rest. Let's say at the end of the month."

"Thank you, sir."

"You're welcome, Ashley. You're a good man."

Bill Ashley smiled when he shook hands, for how would Smith know if he were a good man or an atrocious misfit? Peculiar fellow, that Smith, with his fear of the sun. The only other one-way windows Ashley knew of were at the Langley headquarters of the CIA and Washington headquarters of NSA.

With the Smith formality taken care of, Ashley put in the proper forms to his real boss in Washington. The answer was yes.

As was custom, he was taken off sensitive matters right away and just did garbage work waiting for his vacation. On the day before departure he transferred his savings account into his checking account. He would have liked to have given Mr. Winch the cash directly, but if his real boss got word—and they had people who would give them the word—that Ashley had withdrawn $8,000 from his savings in cash just before his vacation out of the country, there would be more government people around him than ants on a piece of sugar. He was sure Mr. Winch would take a check. He would have to. That's all Ashley had.

"Brandy snifter," said Mr. Winch when Ashley was shown into the coldest heated room this side of outdoors—the lord's chambers of Kildonan, it was called—"you must first wait until your check clears. A check is a promise of money. It is not money."

When the check did clear, Ashley quickly wished it hadn't, so badly did his back and arms hurt from

12

waiting in the position of respect on the cold wooden floor. And for $20,000 he wasn't even getting a private lesson. There were three others in the class.

They were a bit younger than Ashley and a bit more athletic and much more advanced. Mr. Winch made Ashley watch. Their strokes seemed familiar, yet much simpler. The circling motions were much tighter than Ashley had seen anywhere else, not so much a fixed circle but the forcing of a turn around an opponent.

"You see, Mr. Ashley, you were trained to practice you circling motions around an imaginary point," Winch explained. "Your method was learned from someone a long time ago who watched this method in practice, probably against someone who didn't move. Sometimes it works, sometimes it doesn't. That is because it is derivative. All the derivative arts have their flaws because they copy the externals without understanding the essence. And there are other reasons. Witness the kung fu masters who attempted to fight Thai boxers. Not one survived the first round. Why?"

Just to relieve the building pressure on his back from the fixed position, Ashley raised a hand. Mr. Winch nodded.

"Because they had not been trained to fight but to pretend to fight," said Ashley.

"Very good," said Mr. Winch. "But more importantly, the boxers were hard men winnowed from the soft. The boxers had used their skills for their living. The boxers were at work; the kung fu at play. Up, Ashley, on your feet. Assume a position."

"Which position, Mr. Winch?"

"Any position, brandy snifter. Stand or crouch or

13

hide. You'd be better off with a gun, probably, and perhaps two hundred yards distance. That is, if you had a gun, which I wouldn't give you."

"What am I supposed to be learning?"

"That a fool and his life are soon parted."

Mr. Winch clapped his hands and a large, blond, crewcut man, with a hard face and ice blue eyes and hands with knuckles meshed together, danced forward and came into Bill Ashley hard. He also came fast. Ashley didn't see the blow, and he knew he had been hit only when he tried to move his left arm. It wouldn't.

The next man, a big bear of muscle and hair, giggled as he took out Ashley's right arm. It felt as if his shoulders had two hot knives attached to them, and suddenly Bill Ashley realized he needed his arms for balance. It was very hard to stand, and then it was even harder when the left leg went and he was down on the floor writhing and moaning his agony, after the third trainee had delivered the leg blow.

And then the right leg went when Mr. Winch immobilized it with a disdainful kick.

Ashley screamed when they took off his white gi. The bones must be broken, he thought. This was wrong. You didn't break someone's bones in training. That was wrong training. He saw a rice paper banner flutter from the ceiling, and he knew by the cold at his back that someone was opening a window. It was not his imagination. It was getting colder. He knew his clothing was off, but he could not look. His head had to stay exactly where it was or his joints felt incredible pain, as if someone were shredding his ligaments with a rasp.

14

He saw the banner on the ceiling float down, a lop-sided upside-down trapezoid with a vertical line through it. A simple symbol he had never seen before.

"Why? Why? Why?" moaned Bill Ashley, softly, for loud talk made his arms move slightly.

"Because you work at Folcroft, brandy snifter," he heard Mr. Winch say. It was too painful to turn his head to look at Winch.

"Then it wasn't for my money."

"Of course it was for your money."

"But Folcroft?"

"It was because of Folcroft, too. But money is always nice, brandy snifter. You have been poorly taught. From your very hello to the world, you have been coming to this day because you were poorly taught. Goodbye, brandy snifter, you were never made for the martial arts."

There was one blessing to the chill that overcame his bare body on the new wooden floor in the lord's chambers of Kildonan Castle. It was going to make everything better. Already, his pain was numbing and soon it would all be gone. The temperature fell further at night and Ashley slipped into a deep darkness, only to be disappointed by weak light in the morning. But when the room was most light, about the time of the high sun, Ashley slipped again into the deep darkness, and this time he did not come out.

He was found six days later by a detective from Scotland Yard acting on a tip from a telephone caller who would later be described as having a "vaguely Oriental" voice.

The yard also got Ashley's New York State, U.S.A., driver's license in the mail without a note.

15

Since it was addressed to the detective who got the tip, he assumed the body belonged to William Ashley, 38, 855 Pleasant Lane, Rye, N.Y., five-feet-ten, 170 pounds, brown eyes, brown hair, mole on left hand, no corrective lenses.

It not only checked out, it became known as the "Kildonan Castle Murder," and the detective appeared on the telly describing the gruesomeness of the death and how the yard was looking for a madman.

Ashley had died of exposure, not of the broken limbs, each shattered at the joint, he said. No, there were no clues. But the murder scene was horrid. Frightfully horrid. Yes, he could be quoted on that. Frightfully horrid. Never seen anything like it before.

It was when he had finished his second daily press briefing that the man from British Intelligence had all those questions.

"Did this Ashley fellow take long to die?"

"Yessir. He died of exposure."

"Were any papers found on him?"

"No sir. The bloke was stark raving nude. Exposure will kill faster than thirst or hunger."

"Yes, we're well aware of that. Was there any indication that he was tortured for information?"

"Well, sir, leaving a person with four crushed limbs naked on a bare, cold floor in a drafty highland castle is not exactly a comfort-inducing experience, wouldn't you say, sir?"

"You don't know, is that right?"

"Correct, sir. Was this chap important in some way?"

"Really, now, that's not something you'd expect me to answer, is it?"

16

"No, sir."

"Did you find out who had title to the castle?"

"British government, sir. Castle was abandoned for taxes years ago. Owner couldn't keep it up, so to speak."

"Which means what?"

"Unoccupied, sir."

"I see. Are you telling me ghosts did it?"

"No sir."

"Very good. We'll get back to you. And forget you spoke to me, would you please?"

"Forgotten already, sir."

The report by British intelligence to the American Embassy in London was brief. Ashley had come to England as a tourist, had proceeded directly to Scotland, spent one evening at a small inn and was then discovered more than a week later in a condition of semidismemberment.

It was a closed coffin funeral in Rye, New York. Which was an excellent idea since the body was not that of William Ashley but a derelict from the New York city morgue. The Ashley body was in a medical school just outside Chicago where a doctor who thought he worked for the Central Intelligence Agency was examining the limbs. The blows, more than likely, had been made by some sort of sledge-hammer. The joints were too shattered for the human hand to have inflicted the damage. Ashley had indeed died of exposure, contracting pneumonia with the lungs filling and causing death somewhat akin to drowning.

In Rye, New York, an agent who believed he was working undercover for the FBI, posing as an agent of a federal reserve board, saw to it that the $8,000 missing from the Ashley savings account was redeposited with no record that it had ever been withdrawn.

And the only person who knew exactly what all these men were doing and why sat behind a desk in Folcroft Santarium, looking out his one-way windows at Long Island Sound, hoping Ashley had indeed been a victim of robbery.

He had ordered the $8,000 put back into the account because the last thing this incident needed was more international publicity with Ashley's wife crying about missing money. The National Security Agency had been a bit lax in not having reported the transfer of Ashley's funds from savings to checking, but by and large it was the most thorough and accurate of all the country's services.

Dr. Harold Smith, the man whom Ashley thought was his cover, was the only man who knew what Ashley did for a living. Including Ashley.

He reviewed the man's program files. Ashley had been in charge of storing information on East Coast shipping. He had thought he was heading an information sorting, which tried to detect foreign penetration of national shipping, always a key spot for espionage. But Ashley's real function, which he could never see because he only performed half of it, was tabulating real shipping incomes versus ladings.

It was part of an overall formula Dr. Smith had worked out years before that showed, when ladings began to exceed income, that organized crime was gaining too much control over the waterfronts.

Smith had found out years before that he could not

18

end crime's influence on the waterfront, which included everything from loansharking to the unions. But what he could do was to keep crime from controlling shipping. When the formula showed that that was becoming a danger, a district attorney would suddenly get proof of kickbacks at the ports or the Internal Revenue Service would get xeroxed copies of bills of sales for a shipping executive who bought $200,000 homes on a $22,000 a year salary.

Ashley never knew this. He just worked on feeding the computer core. His terminal couldn't even get a readout without registering it up in Dr. Smith's office. Smith checked the records. The last time Ashley had requested a readout of the computer was six months before, and that was merely to check the accuracy of some data he had fed in the day before.

Going over it for the last time, Smith had to conclude that if William Ashley had been tortured to the last secret hiding place of his mind, he could not tell his captors what he did for a living. He simply could not know.

No one in the organization knew what it was that he did for a living—no one, but two.

It had all been carefully arranged like that years before. It was the essence of the organization, formed more than a decade before by a now dead president who had called Smith to his office and told him the United States government did not work.

"Under the Constitution, we cannot control organized crime. We cannot control revolutionaries. There are so many things we cannot control if we live by the Constitution. Yet, if we do not extend some measure of control, they will destroy this country. They will lead it to chaos," said the sandy-haired young man with the Boston accent. "And chaos leads to a dictatorship. As surely as water falls over a dam, a lack of order leads to too much order. We're doomed unless . . ."

And the "unless" that Smith heard was an organization set up outside the Constitution, outside the government, an organization that did not exist, set up to try to keep the government alive.

The organization would last for a short while, no more than two years, and then disappear, never seeing public light. And Smith would head it.

Smith had a question. Why him?

Because, the President had explained, in his years of service, Smith, more than any other manager in the Central Intelligence Agency, had showed a lack of prideful ambition.

"All the psychological tests show you would never use this organization to take over the country. Frankly, Dr. Smith, you have what can be uncharitably described as an incredible lack of imagination."

"Yes," Smith had said. "I know. It's always been like that. My wife complains sometimes."

"It's your strength," said the President. "Something amazed me though, and I'm going to ask you about it now because we will never see each other again, and you will of course forget this meeting . . ."

"Of course," Smith interrupted.

"What puzzles me, Dr. Smith, is how on earth you could flunk a Rorschach test. It's in your aptitude records."

"Oh, that," Smith said. "I remember. I saw ink blots."

20

"Right. And in a Rorschach test, you're supposed to describe what the blots look like."

"I did, Mr. President. They looked like ink blots."

And that was how it had started. The organization was supposed to be an information-gathering and -dispensing operation, providing prosecutors with information, letting newspapers get stories to embarrass corrupt officials. But early on it became apparent that information was not enough. The organization that did not exist needed a killer arm. It needed a killer arm the size of a small army, but small armies had many mouths and you didn't very well convince a hit man he worked for the Department of Agriculture. They needed an extraordinary single killer who didn't exist—for an organization that didn't exist.

It was really rather simple at first.

The organization had found the man it wanted working in a small police department in New Jersey, and it had framed him for a murder he didn't commit, and it had electrocuted him in an electric chair that didn't work, and when he came to he was officially a dead man. Such was his nature, which had been scrupulously checked out before, that he took well to working for the organization and learned well from his Oriental trainer, becoming—but for a few small character flaws—the perfect human weapon.

Smith thought about this as he watched a storm brew darkly over the Long Island Sound. He fingered Ashley's file. Something did not fit. The method of killing was so insane, it just might have a special purpose and meaning.

Everything else about the case had seemed orderly, even to the withdrawal of the money. The killing

21

came after the check had been cashed through a Swiss bank account in the name of a Mr. Winch. Smith examined again the report from British intelligence. Ashley had been killed on a freshly finished wooden floor. So heavy machinery had not been used to crush his limbs because its marks would have showed on the floor. Perhaps light machinery? Perhaps the killer was a sadist?

For a man who not only did not believe in hunches, but could not quite remember ever having one, Dr. Harold W. Smith felt a strange sensation when thinking about the Ashley death. There had been a purpose to the way he was killed. Smith didn't know why he thought that, but nevertheless he kept thinking it.

Through his evening meal of codfish cake and lukewarm succotash, he thought about it. Through his perfunctory goodnight kiss to his wife, he thought about it. In the morning he thought about it even while processing other matters.

And since it was beginning to interfere with his other duties, which could lead to disruption in the entire organization, it therefore demanded an answer.

And it had to be quickly because, of the two men who might be able to answer the riddle of Ashley's death, one was on an assignment and the other was preparing to return home to a small village in North Korea.

CHAPTER TWO

His name was Remo and the fresh snow fell on his open hand and he felt the flakes pile up. At the edge of the tall pine tree, across the three hundred yards to the yellow light coming from the cabin, was fresh, white, even snow, not even drifting in the windless late autumn evening in Burdette, Minnesota.

Remo had walked to the edge of the clearing, circling the cabin until he was sure. Now he knew. The perfect clearing in the Minnesota woods was an open field of fire. The assistant attorney general had made sure of that. If he didn't see anyone coming, then his dog would smell them, and from that cabin, anyone coming across that open blanket of white, by ski, by snowshoe, foot by foot, anyone would be almost a stationary target in the yellow light cutting the November night.

For some reason, Remo thought back to a night more than a decade before when he was strapped into an electric chair, when he thought he had died, and then had awakened to a new life as a man whose fingerprints had gone into the dead file, a man who did not exist for an organization that did not exist.

But Remo knew something that his boss, Dr. Harold W. Smith, did not know. He *had* died in that electric chair. The person who had been Remo Williams died, because the years of training had been so intense that even Remo's nervous system had changed and he had changed, so that now he was someone else.

Remo noticed the snow melt in his hand and he smiled. When you lost concentration, you lost it all. If he let the whole thing go, he would next feel chill in his body and then, out here in the freezing Minnesota snow, he would surrender his body to the elements and die. Cold was not a fixed point on a thermometer but the relationship between the body and its environment.

An old children's trick was putting one hand under hot running water and the other hand under cold water, and then plunging both hands into a bowl of lukewarm water. To the hand which had been hot, the lukewarm water felt cold. To the hand that had been cold, the lukewarm water felt hot. So too with temperature's effects on the body. Up to a certain point, it was not the temperature of the body, but the difference between the outside temperature and the body's temperature. And if the body temperature could be lowered, then a man could stand subfreezing weather in a light white sweater and white gym pants and white leather sneakers, and a man could hold a snowflake in his hand and watch it not melt.

Remo felt the quiet of the snow and saw gusts of sparks come out of the chimney of the yellow-lit cabin far off.

Snow was very light water, water with more oxygen in it, and if you let your body into it, moving level with the ground and it was all around you and you were part of its whiteness, not an intrusion on top of it, but every portion of your body moving through it, then it became light water and you moved quickly,

24

not breathing, but with fingers darting forward and flattened palms pushing back and the body going level and quickly toward where the cabin had last been seen above the snow.

Remo stopped and his knees automatically lowered, packing the snow beneath them. He lifted his head above the opaque whiteness and smelled the fresh burning hickory and the heavy, fatty odor of meat cooking. Two figures moved behind the steamed windows. One jerky and the other with the hollow float of a woman, probably young. The assistant attorney general did have a girlfriend, Smith had told Remo, and of course there could be no living witnesses. From what Remo had gathered, the assistant attorney general had the incredible misfortune to come into certain cases prepared badly. Prosecution witnesses wound up proving a defendant's innocence; legal procedures fouled up so that so many criminals' rights were violated that they never went on trial.

Many, many mistakes which Assistant Attorney General Dawkins would blame on the courts for being too soft. And while other lawyers grew rich by preparing their cases, James Bellamy Dawkins became even richer by not preparing his.

It was when a mousy title clerk who thought she earned her side income from the National Real Estate Annual filed her yearly report with the magazine—which somehow rarely published anything she sent—that James Bellamy Dawkins was on his way to targethood.

A computer in a Long Island sanitarium on Long Island Sound spit out these coupled facts: Lost cases increased riches. In the instance of James Bellamy

Dawkins, the worse he did in court, the more land he owned.

It was put to him somewhat gently at first. Perhaps, having two more years to serve and having already accumulated a sizeable fortune, he might want to devote his full energies to convicting certain perpetrators. He was shown a list that remarkably coincided with his benefactors.

He rejected the suggestion with a warning that should anyone attempt to remove him from office, he would immediately indict everyone on that list for abundant crimes they could not have committed, and when the charges were dropped, let them sue the state of Minnesota silly.

Better yet, indict them for murdering his caller and once they were acquitted, they could go out and do the real thing because a man couldn't be tried for the same crime twice.

In brief, Assistant Attorney General James Bellamy Dawkins was not going to change his ways nor was he going to resign, and God help the state if anyone tried to push him out.

That response ultimately reached the Folcroft computer and gave all those facts to Dr. Harold W. Smith, who decided immediately that America could do without James Bellamy Dawkins.

So Remo's eyes rose above the snowline and he saw the two figures and smelled the cabin smells and lowered his head back into the whiteness where his knees rose and he moved forward, not packing the very light water in which he went, but moving through it as if he belonged to it.

Remo heard the dogs bark and the cabin door open

crisply and a man's voice say, "What is it, Queenie?"
And Queenie barked.

"I don't see anything, Queenie," came the voice
again.

And just because he felt like it and just because he
had seen a horror movie recently and possibly because
it was Halloween, Remo poked a little hole up
through the snow and moaned:

"James Bellamy Dawkins, your days are num-
bered."

"Who the hell is that?"

"James Bellamy Dawkins, you will not live through
the night."

"You there. Wherever you are. I can blow your
head off."

"Trick or treat," said Remo.

"Where are you?"

"Trick or treat," said Remo.

"Go get him, Queenie."

Remo heard the barking approach and Dawkins, a
paunchy man with hollow face and a .30-30 rifle at
rest in front of him, saw his bull mastiff streak
through the snow, her body leaving a beveled path,
her feet churning cones spaced at the outside of the
bevel. When Queenie grabbed hold of whatever it
was, she would get a good piece of him and Dawkins
would shoot away the rest. The man obviously had
come to kill him and all Dawkins had to do to show
self-defense was to make sure a weapon was found on
the body. If it didn't have one, he would supply it.
The man was already on his property and that would
suffice as circumstantial evidence supporting intent.
The weapon would do the rest.

But a strange thing happened to Queenie, who had already devoured her fill of fall rabbits and had even come out on top against a family of raccoons. The path she made suddenly ended and she disappeared in the snow. Vanished.

Dawkins raised the gun to his shoulder and blasted around the area the dog had silently disappeared into. He heard a moan and he fired the lever action rifle again and the next shot showed the snow darkening and he chuckled to himself.

"What the hell are you shooting at, Jimmy?" came a woman's voice from inside the cabin.

"Shut up, honey," said Dawkins.

"What you shooting at this time of night?"

"Nothing. Shut up and go to bed."

Dawkins aimed at the spot where the red darkness was beginning to spread and he saw a small convulsion under the snow. Somehow the man had made his way under the fresh snowfall, but he saw no declivity leading to the blood, just Queenie's trail.

He watched and the snow was still, and then he tramped out from the cabin to inspect his kill. But when he was almost to where Queenie had gone out of sight, he felt something tugging at the back of his pants and he found his body sitting down. Then a hand was smacking snow into his face and he could not hold onto his .30-30 and he tried desperately to get the snow out of his face.

He tried to stand, but just when a foot seemed to get firmness underneath it, it somehow slid out. When he tried brushing the snow from his mouth, his hand seemed to go out in strange directions. Then the horror of it overtook him.

He was going to drown in snow and he could neither stand nor get the cold air-draining stuff out of his mouth. Then, in one last desperate life-grabbing thrust, he threw his whole body away from the force that seemed to be holding him down. And he moved nowhere and swallowed another handful of snow.

Everything became white and then he was no longer cold. Only his body was. When he was discovered the next morning by his horrified mistress, the county coroner labeled his death suicide. As he figured it, Dawkins had "flipped his giggy," shot his dog, then rolled around swallowing snow until he drowned and froze.

In Minnesota, the incident made immediate headlines:

ELECTED OFFICIAL DEAD IN LOVE NEST

By the time the story was in print, Remo's plane had landed at Raleigh Durham Airport in North Carolina where he took a taxi to a motel outside Chapel Hill.

"Out all night?" winked the desk clerk.

"Sort of," said Remo.

The desk clerk chuckled. "You must have spent it indoors. Nights can get chilly here in late autumn."

"I wasn't cold," said Remo honestly.

"Oh, I wish I were young again," said the clerk.

"Young has got nothing to do with it," said Remo, taking three keys because he had rented three adjoining rooms.

"There was a call for you from your Uncle Marvin."

"At what time?"

" 'Bout ten-thirty this morning. Funny thing happened. The phone went dead almost as soon as I rang your room. I went to your door and yelled that there was a phone call but all I heard was the television on inside, and I didn't push it."

"I know you didn't push it," said Remo.

"How's that?"

"You're breathing, aren't you?" said Remo and when he slipped into the middle room he was very quiet because a frail, elderly Oriental with a wispy beard sat on the floor in lotus position, golden kimono draped immaculately around him.

The television set with the taping device to catch the other channels and then run the concurrent shows consecutively so that not one second of one soap opera would be missed was on.

Remo sat down quietly, not even rustling the couch. When Chiun, the Master of Sinanju, was enjoying his daytime dramas, no one, not even his pupil Remo, disturbed him.

In the past, some, by accident, had thought this was just an old man watching soap operas and had failed to treat this moment with reverence. They were no longer among the living.

So Remo sat as Mrs. Lorrie Banks discovered that her young lover loved her for herself and not her new face lift operation performed by Dr. Jennings Bryant, whose eldest daughter had run away with Morton Lancaster, the noted economist, who was being blackmailed by Doretta Daniels, the former belly dancer who had purchased the controlling shares in the Elk Ridge Cancer research hospital, and was threatening

30

to close it down unless Lorrie disclosed where Peter Malthus had parked his car the night Lorrie's eldest daughter was run over and crippled for weeks, during the night of the flood when Captain Rambough Donnester had run away from the dark incident in his past, leaving the entire city of Elk Ridge exposed to the elements without the protection of the Air National Guard.

Lorrie was talking to Dr. Bryant, wondering whether Peter should be told about his mother. It occurred to Remo that just about two years earlier the actress was discussing whether someone else should be told some other gloomy thing about a relative, and what made these dramas different from reality was not so much what happened but that everyone was so all fired concerned about it. To Chiun, however, this was beauty and, as much as anything could be, a justification for American civilization. He was further convinced that this was the epitome of American culture when, in an exchange program with Russia, America had sent the New York Philharmonic—as Chiun said, "keeping the good things home." In exchange, Russia had sent the Bolshoi Ballet, which Chiun knew was also second-rate because their dancers were clumsy.

It was four-thirty in the afternoon when the last commercial on the last show was finished, a movie came on, and Chiun turned off the set.

"I do not like your breathing," he said.

"My breathing is the same as yesterday, Little Father," said Remo.

"That is why I do not like it. It should be quieter within you today."

"Why?"

31

"Because today you are different."

"In what way, Little Father?"

"That is for you to understand. When you do not know how you are each day, then you lose sight of yourself. Know this, no man has ever had two days alike."

"Did we get a phone call from upstairs?"

"There was a rude interruption, but I did not hold it against the maker of the telephone call. I endured the rudeness and the callousness and the lack of consideration for a poor old man enjoying the meager pleasures in the quiet twilight of his life."

Remo looked for the telephone to return the call. He found a hole where the cord had been snapped clean from the wall. He looked for the detached phone and not until he saw a dark hole in the white wood dresser did he realize where the phone had gone. The cracked body of the instrument was imbedded in the back of the dresser, welding the entire piece of furniture to the wall.

Remo went into an adjacent bedroom and dialed a number. This number did not activate a telephone directly, instead it sparked a series of connections across the country, so that there was no single line making up the connection by the time a phone finally did ring in the office of the director of Folcroft Sanitarium.

"Hello," said Remo. "Uncle Nathan called."

"No," said Dr. Smith. "Uncle Marvin called."

"Yeah, right," said Remo. "I knew it was somebody."

"I tried to reach you before, but we were disconnected and I thought you might have been clearing something up at the time."

"No. The phone rang while Chiun was watching his shows."

"Oh," said Smith heavily. "I have sort of a special problem. An accident happened to someone in a rather strange way and I thought you and Chiun might be able to shed some light on it."

"You mean he was killed in a way you don't know and you'd figure Chiun or I would know."

"Remo, please. There's no such thing as a completely secure telephone line."

"Whaddya going to do? Send me a matchbook with invisible ink on it? C'mon, Smitty, I've got more important things in my life than playing security games."

"What is more important in your life, Remo?"

"Breathing correctly. Do you know I'm breathing the same today as yesterday?"

Smith cleared his throat and Remo knew it was the sound of unhappiness, that Smith had heard something he did not wish to deal with because he was afraid that further answers might confuse him more. He knew that Smith had recently given up trying to fathom him and was beginning to accept Remo like Chiun. An unknown quantity that served well. It was a major concession by a man who loathed anything he could not put in some order, well-labeled and perfectly filed. Mysteries were anathema to the head of the organization.

"On second thought," said Smith. "Send your Aunt Mildred a birthday greeting. She's fifty-five tomorrow."

"That means I'm supposed to meet you at O'Hare Airport information at three in the afternoon. Or is it three in the morning? Or is it Logan Airport?"

"Morning. O'Hare," said Smith dourly, and Remo heard the receiver go dead.

On the flight from Raleigh-Durham to Chicago's O'Hare Airport, Chiun suddenly marveled at the hidden skills of Americans. Chiun acknowledged that he should have known that there must be other areas of excellence.

"Any nation that could produce *As the Planet Revolves* or *The Young and the Daring* must have other isolated pockets of worth," said Chiun.

Remo knew that Chiun thought airplanes were very close to soundly designed flying objects, so he commented that America was the leader in aircraft and that he had never heard of a Korean-designed plane.

Chiun ignored that comment.

"What I am talking about," he said grandly, producing two torn pieces of white paper between his long graceful fingernails, "is here. This. And in America, too. What a pleasant surprise to find such an art so well performed in a place so far away as America."

Remo looked at the sheets. They were filled single space with sloppy typing.

"This, one can trust. I sent him my birthday and place and time of birth to the exact minute, and I sent him yours."

"You don't know for sure when I was born. Neither do I," said Remo. "The orphanage records weren't that exact."

With a flurry, Chiun's hands dismissed Remo's reservations as inconsequential.

"Even with an inexact date, such excellence of accuracy," said Chiun.

34

Remo looked closer. On the other side of the papers were circles with strange signs in them.

"What is it?" asked Remo.

"An astrology chart," said Chiun. "And in America, too. I am most pleasantly surprised that the great art, so poorly practiced by so many, is done well and in, of all places, America."

"I don't buy that stuff," said Remo.

"Of course, because in America little machines do everything in quantity. But you forget that men of brilliance and insight still exist. You do not believe in the forces of the universe because you have seen fools and charlatans represent them. But there is in America at least one true reader of the planets."

"Dippy dong," said Remo and winked at a passing stewardess, who almost dropped her tray in pleasant surprise. Remo knew he should not have done that because invariably the stewardess would be at him all trip for coffee, tea, milk, pillow for his head, magazines, and anything else that would get her close to him. At New York's Kennedy, two years before, a Pan-Am lassie had followed him from the plane crying that he had left a Kleenex in the seat.

"You may say that," said Chiun, "but let me read to you in your own language the keen insights of this reader of the forces of the universe."

And Chiun read in the manner of story-telling with his voice rising on the significant points and lowering at the serious ones.

"You," read Chiun, "are in tune with the gentleness and beauty of your world. Few realize your wisdom and kindness that is concealed by your desire for humility. You are troubled by the incessant badgering of

35

those close to you who cannot publicly acknowledge your awesome magnificence."

"Pretty good," said Remo. "And what did he write about you?"

"That is me," said Chiun, and he read from the other paper: "You have a tendency to self-indulgence and are wont to function on whatever thought passes through your mind. You do not think things through, but run through days as if you have no tomorrow."

"That's me, I take it," said Remo glumly.

"To the letter," said Chiun. "Oh, does he know you. There is more. 'You do not appreciate the great gifts given you and squander them like duck droppings.'"

"Where?" said Remo. "Let me see where he said that. Where did he say 'duck droppings'?"

"He didn't say that exactly. But he would have if he knew you better."

"I see," said Remo, and asked for the two papers. True. All but the duck droppings was there. But Remo noticed something else. Chiun's chart started under the heading "positive" and then was torn off midpage. Remo's began under "negatives" and did not have a top of the page.

"You took my negatives and your positives," said Remo.

"I kept that which was correct. There is enough misinformation in the world. Let us be grateful that, in a country like this, we have found at least what is half correct."

"Who is this guy?"

"He is the Ke'Gan of the mountains. The mountains always have the best seers. A Ke'Gan. Here in

America. That is why I first chose to write him, telling him of our birth signs." Remo looked at Chiun's chart which still had the astrology service's masthead.

"Ke'Gan?" he said. "The guy's name is Kegan. Brian Kegan. Pittsfield, Massachusetts."

"The Berkshire Mountains," said Chiun.

"Pittsfield. You've still got that post office box there, don't you? What are you doing with a post office box in Pittsfield, Massachusetts? What does a Master of Sinanju need that for?"

But Chiun folded his hands and was silent. The post office box had been rented long before, when Chiun had been ready to take up job offers, so that his assassin's profession could continue to support the aged and the weak and the poor, of his little village of Sinanju in North Korea. But the job crisis had ended and Chiun continued working for Dr. Smith, but he kept the post office box and refused to tell Remo what mail he received there.

The stewardess was back. No. Remo did not want coffee. He did not want tea. He did not want an alcoholic beverage or *Time* Magazine.

"Sir," said the stewardess. "I've never said this to a passenger before, but I bet you think you're something special. I bet you think every woman is just dying to fall in bed with you, doncha?"

Her pale cheeks flushed red and her blonde short-cut bobbed in anger. Remo could smell her delicate perfume. He shrugged.

"I wouldn't have you on a bet, buddy. Not on a bet."

"Oh," said Remo. She left with her pillow and magazines but was back momentarily. She wanted to apologize. She had never talked to a passenger like that before. She was sorry. Remo said it was all right.

"I'd like to make it up somehow."

"Forget it," said Remo.

"I dearly would. Is there any way I could? Just tell me and I'll do it. Whatever you say."

"Forget it," said Remo.

"Screw you," she said. And Chiun, seeing passengers stare, raised a graceful hand, the fingernails a symphony of delicacy.

"Precious blossom, do not belabor your gracious heart. One cannot expect the rodents of the field to appreciate the precious emerald. Do not offer your gracious gift to him who is unworthy."

"You're damned right," said the stewardess. "You got a lot of wisdom there, sir. You really do."

"What did I do?" said Remo, shrugging.

"Go back to your cheese, mouse," said the stewardess. She left with a triumphant smile.

"What came over her?" asked Remo.

"I have given the best years of my life to a fool," said Chiun.

"I didn't want to bang her. So?"

"So you took her pride and she could not leave until it was given back to her."

"I'm under no obligation to service every woman who comes along."

"You are under an obligation not to hurt those who do you no harm."

"Since when is a Master of Sinanju a spreader of love and light?"

"I have always been. But light to a blind man can,

at best, only mean heat. Oh, how the Ke'Gan knows you."

"Let him try turning off your soap operas one time. He'll get your love and light."

CHAPTER THREE

Smith was looking at his watch and waiting like any other piece of dry furniture when Remo and Chiun arrived at the seat opposite the Trans World Airlines ticket counter.

"You're on time," he said to Remo, and to Chiun he gave a curt nod which might be interpreted as a small bow if one did not know that Smith was completely devoid of bows or any other sort of pleasantry. Courtesy required minute amounts of imagination and was therefore impossible for Dr. Harold W. Smith.

The Donsheim Memorial Hospital, perhaps the most modern in the entire Chicago area, was on the outskirts of the city in the pleasant suburbs of Hickory Hills, away from the knifings, shootings, and muggings of the inner city, which desperately needed a supermodern facility like Donsheim and therefore, by the laws of nature and politics, had no chance of ever getting one.

Smith walked around the hospital on the neat, grasslined concrete walk until he came to a gray door without a handle. It had only a lock, and Smith produced a key from a large keychain.

"One of your outlets?" asked Remo.

"In a way," said Smith.

"Everything is in a way," said Remo.

"The emperor knows the emperor's business," said Chiun, to whom anyone who employed the House of

Sinanju was an emperor, as they had been in ages past. It was a breach of propriety that an assassin should talk openly to an emperor, which Remo understood to really mean that an emperor should never know what his assassin was thinking, a practical code worked out over centuries of experience.

Yet Remo was an American and Smith was an American, and just as some things of Sinanju might always remain a mystery to Remo, this openness between Remo and Smith was just as strange to Chiun.

The sharp smell of a hospital corridor brought back memories of fear to Remo, fear he had learned before he knew how to use his nerves for his own power. Smith counted doors, seven in all, and entered the eighth with another key. It was a chilly room, and Smith turned on the lights and buttoned the top button of his coat, shivering. Remo and Chiun stood still in their light autumn clothes. Eight large metal squares with handles stood neatly stacked against the wall. A sharp yellow fluorescent light cast a foreboding glare against the metal.

In the center of the room with white tile floors, smooth for easy scrubbing, were three bare tables, seven feet long and three feet wide with white plastic tops. The disinfectant could not hide it, the constant scrubbing could not hide it, nor could the chill eliminate it. The room smelled of the rot of death, that sickly sweet richness of fatty nodes decomposing and bacteria-heavy intestines dissolving themselves.

"He's in the third one up," said Smith.

Remo rolled out the drawer to the center table.

"William Ashley, thirty-eight, died of exposure," said Smith, looking at the bloated corpse. Facial hair

41

had grown a stubble of beard through the slick dead skin. The eyes bulged under lids that reflected the fluorescent light above. The shoulders bulged as if Ashley had a giant's muscles there, and the hips swelled as if they wore football padding.

"We found through X-rays that all four main joints, shoulders and legs, were damaged. Victim's lungs had filled with fluid caused by exposure. Was found on a bare floor of a chilly Highland castle, unable to move because of joint injuries. In brief, gentlemen, he drowned from his own lung fluids," said Smith. He thrust his hands into his pockets for warmth and continued. "He was one of our employees. What I want to know is do you recognize the method of killing?"

"Cruelty has many forms and many faces. It is unfair to blame the House of Sinanju," said Chiun. "We are known for quietness and swiftness, nay, even for mercy in the speed with which we perform our duties. Kinder than nature we are and have been and always will be."

"Nobody was accusing your house," said Smith. "We want to know if you recognize the manner of death. I know that our methods of concealment and secrecy are confusing to you, but this man was one who worked for us and did not know it, like most of our employees."

"It is very hard to teach servants to know their job," said Chiun. "I am sure that, with the wisdom of Emperor Smith, within but a short time the laggardly servants shall know what they are doing and for whom they work."

42

"Not exactly," said Smith. "We do not wish them to know for whom they work."

"A wise idea. The less an ungrateful and stupid servant knows, the better. You are most wise, Emperor Smith. A credit to your race."

Smith cleared his throat and Remo smiled. Remo was the only man who bridged the gap between the two older men. Remo understood that Smith was trying to explain that there was a force America was ashamed to admit existed, while Chiun believed an emperor should always remind his subjects what forces he had, the stronger the better.

"In any case," Smith said, "this matter bothers me. The strangeness of the death raises some questions and I'd like some answers."

"One cannot blame the House of Sinanju for every cruelty that happens," said Chiun. "Where did this occur?"

"Scotland," said Smith.

"Ah yes, a noble kingdom. A Master of Sinanju has not set foot there for hundreds of years. A fair and gracious people. Like yourself. Of much nobility are they."

"What I'm asking is do you recognize the manner of death? You'll notice the skin hasn't been broken but there has been incredible damage to the joints."

"To three joints," said Remo, "and that was because they didn't know what they were doing."

"I have X-rays," said Smith. "But the doctor who examined the body said all four joints were crushed. I remember that."

"He's wrong," said Remo. "Both shoulders and the right hip are crushed. Sloppy hits. The left leg was the

43

way it should have been done. The leg was taken out without destroying the joint."

Smith set his lips tightly and took a plain gray envelope from his pocket. The X-rays had been reduced in size to look like .35 millimeter film. Smith held the film strips up to the overhead light.

"Gracious. You're right, Remo," he said.

"He has been taught well," said Chiun.

"So you recognize the manner of death?" asked Smith.

"Sure. Somebody who didn't know what he was doing," said Remo. "He got in a good lucky shot on the left leg, and then botched the job on the right hip and both shoulders."

Chiun was looking down at William Ashley's body, and he was shaking his head.

"There were at least two people who did this thing," he said. "The one who was correct in the left leg, and whoever else did the other work of butchery. Who was this person?"

"An employee," said Smith. "A computer programmer."

"And why would one wish to disgrace this whatever-you-said?"

"Computer programmer," said Smith.

"Correct. That is the word. Why would one wish to disgrace him?"

"I don't know," said Smith.

"Then I know nothing about the way of death," said Chiun.

"That doesn't help, Chiun," said Smith with a slight trace of exasperation. "What should we do?"

"Watch everything closely," answered Chiun, who

44

knew that Americans liked to watch their disasters to give them a good headstart, until even the most dense person in the land realized something was wrong.

And then Chiun brought up something that had been bothering him. He had been promised a visit to his home. He knew it was a difficult journey and that it would cost much to deliver him to Sinanju. All was in preparedness even to the special boat that would slip him into Sinanju Harbor from under the water. But he had not gone at the time it was first ready because of his loyalty to Emperor Smith, long might he reign in the glory that was uniquely his.

"Yes, the submarine," said Smith.

Humbly, Chiun requested that he leave now for his visit. Korea in the late autumn was beautiful.

"Sinanju is freezing, windy ice in late Autumn," said Remo who had never been there.

"It is home," said Chiun.

"I know that is the home of the House of Sinanju," said Smith, "and you have served well. You have done wonders with Remo. It is a pleasure to assist you in returning you home to your village. But we will have difficulty in sending your shows to you. You might have to do without your television shows."

"I shall not be in Sinanju long," said Chiun. "Just until Remo gets there."

"I'd hate to have both of you out of the country," said Smith.

"Don't worry, I'm not going," said Remo.

"He will be there by the next full moon," said Chiun, and he said no more until the next day when he was preparing to board a plane that would take

45

him to San Diego where his special ship would take him home.

Chiun waited until Smith had gone to a booth to buy insurance on Chiun's life, before he told Remo:

"That manner of death, Remo, it is very strange."

"Why strange?" said Remo. "A duffer with one lucky hit and three bad ones."

"There is a custom in Sinanju. When you wish to disgrace someone, to show that he is not even worth the killing, the ancient custom is to deliver four blows, then walk away and let your opponent die."

"You think that's what happened here?" Remo.

"I do not know what happened here, but I tell you to be careful until you join me in Sinanju."

"I'm not coming, Little Father," insisted Remo.

"By the next full moon," said Chiun, and then he signed the insurance form Smith put in his hands with a complicated ideograph that looked like the word IF drawn between two parallel lines.

As Chiun's plane took off, Smith said, "A mysterious man."

"Mysterious is just a western term for rude and thoughtless," said Remo as he felt the chill from nearby Lake Michigan whip over the guard rail at O'Hare.

"Mysterious is my term for what you and he are able to accomplish, what you do. For instance, without using guns."

Remo watched the white painted 707 with the stripes of red thrust into the air, its jets bellowing heat and smoke.

"It's not that complicated when you know," he said. "It makes a lot of sense. It's simple when you

46

know, but in its execution it can be complicated. Especially in its simplicity."

"That's not really clear," said Smith.

"Look at him," said Remo as he saw the plane circle. "Look at him. Just going home like that. Well, I guess he's got a right to."

"You didn't say why you didn't use a gun."

"A gun sends a missile. Your hands are more controlled."

"Your hands are. But it's not karate, is it, or one of those?"

"No," said Remo. "Not one of those." Chicago was a cold and lonely place.

"Why you? Why Chiun? What makes you different?"

The plane too quickly became a speck. "What?" asked Remo.

"Why are you two so effective? I've had comparison readouts done with the martial arts, and once in a while there is an isolated instance of one of the things you do, but by and large it's just nothing like what you do."

"Oh, that," said Remo. "The guys with the wooden boards and their hands and stuff like that."

"Stuff like that," said Smith.

"Well, I'll try to explain," said Remo, and he explained as well as he could, as well as he had tried to explain it to himself. For he had not learned it in terms of almost anything he had known before meeting the Master of Sinanju.

First, the main difference might be the simple comparison of a professional football player and a touch football player. An injury that would send a Sunday

47

touch passer to the sidelines wouldn't even be felt by a linebacker in the National Football League.

"The pro does it for his living. It's beyond those levels of entertainment or even ambition. It's survival. The pro lives by what he does. There's no comparison. The second is Sinanju itself. It was, like, born out of desperation. I've heard it from Chiun. Farming and fishing were so poor in that village that they had to drown their own babies."

"I know that the Masters of Sinanju supported their village by renting themselves out," Smith said. "Frankly, with the communists in North Korea I thought that might end."

"Well, it might end in fact, but where Sinanju started, the method and the thought, was every Master knowing it was the life of his target or the life of his village's children. Every Master. For thousands of years. Down to Chiun."

"Okay," said Smith. "For them, survival. But why your high competence?"

"Well, in learning, the Masters of Sinanju found out that most human muscles were on their way to becoming vestigial organs like the appendix. They learned that most everyone uses maybe ten percent of his strength or intelligence or what have you. Chiun's secret is teaching the muscles and nerves and stuff to use maybe thirty per cent. Or forty."

"That's what he does? Forty percent?"

"That's what I do," said Remo. "Chiun's the Master of Sinanju. He does one hundred per cent. On his bad days."

"And that's the explanation?"

"That's the explanation," said Remo, turning from

48

the guardrail. "As to whether it's the truth, I don't have the vaguest. It's the way I explain it."

"I see," said Smith.

"No, you don't," said Remo. "And you never will."

CHAPTER FOUR

When Hawley Bardwell killed his first man with his hands, he knew he had to kill another. It was not like his first tackle in a football game where he heard the knee of the halfback pop in his ear. That was good. But to see a man going to die when you hit him with just your hand was beyond satisfaction.

It was like discovering you had this tremendous need only when it had been filled, and then, in a rush of feeling so good, Bardwell had stepped back on the bare, new polished wooden floor of that drafty castle and watched the black belt guy spin backward, reaching to support the shoulder that would never move again.

It was so simple it was laughable. The guy, named Ashley something, Bill Ashley or Ashley Williams or whatever, had taken that *sanchin-dachi* stance and had made a simple block, and then the left blocking arm itself was used to crack back into the joint. With the first pain of that, Bardwell had his second stroke right into the joint, and that was the beginning. Of course, he didn't have that guy all to himself. He had to share him, but he knew it was his blow that started it and when they left the guy squirming on the floor, that cold floor, pinned by the pain in his own joints, Bardwell knew football, karate, even three years boxing professionally, was like 3.2 beer compared to white lightning. It just didn't compare.

So when Mr. Winch promised him his own kill, personal, nobody else to share, Hawley Bardwell almost fell down and kissed his instructor's feet. Mr. Winch was what he had always wanted as a coach or as a commander in the Marines. Mr. Winch understood. Mr. Winch had given him the power. No matter how tempting so far, Hawley Bardwell, six-feet-four of hard knotted muscle and chilling blue eyes and a face that looked as if it were hacked out of a stone wall, kept his hands to their purposes assigned by Mr. Winch.

And when he had to wait by the cemetery in Rye, New York, and when a man who looked like his hit, but really wasn't, came to pay respects to one of the graves, that William Ashley, Hawley Bardwell held back. It was not the man. He was almost six feet tall with high cheekbones and deepset brown eyes, but he didn't have those thick wrists. So Hawley Bardwell waited his week as Mr. Winch had told him, and then drove down to New York City, parking his car in one of those incredibly expensive garages his wife had warned him about, and went to the Waldorf Astoria where he asked for Mr. Sun Yee as Mr. Winch had instructed.

Mr. Sun Yee was, of course, Mr. Winch, who said that he took many names, "Winch" being closest to what his name really was.

"Good afternoon, Mr. Winch," said Bardwell to the shorter man who met him in a shimmering green kimono.

"Come in, Bardwell," said Winch. "I take it you did not see your target."

"Right. How'd ya know?"

51

"I know many things," said Winch and smiled.

Bardwell felt uneasy about the smile, like a tickle in his stomach. If Lynette had not been so specific when they had started their journey to Scotland about Mr. Winch being the best thing—next to her of course—in Hawley's life, he might, even with his great respect, be suspicious of Mr. Winch. Great man, but that smile was something else.

"Well, let's see how much you have remembered," said Mr. Winch and Hawley Bardwell assumed the stance he had been drilled in and then redrilled in, and redrilled in. Knowing enough about the martial arts he knew there were other stances, but Mr. Winch had always said he must get this one right and feeling a hand on his spine, he knew he still didn't have it down perfectly.

This was the stance from which he had struck the blow in the castle. You stood with your weight within yourself, not rested on any foot, not so much evenly distributing the weight, but keeping the weight inside yourself, and being within yourself, you struck from the inside of your weight. From the outside, it looked like someone standing with feet slightly apart, almost slouching, and the blow came pop, first pushing the left-hand block back into your man's shoulder, then following. It sounded like *po-pop* when done right. Standing in the hotel suite, Hawley remembered the delicious sound of his hit's shoulder going *po-pop*.

Mr. Winch clapped and Hawley's big right arm slapped out first flat for the block and then instantly turning into the nukite hand sword it was supposed to be.

52

"Good," said Mr. Winch to Hawley Bardwell who stood with arm outstretched as if shaking hands with someone he didn't wish to get close to. "Very good."

"But this sort of leaves me open, don't it? I mean my whole body is open now. I've been practicing, and everytime I do this stroke, I think how open I am at the end of it."

"To add some protection to you," Mr. Winch said, "would make you less effective. Against the man who will be your target, your defensive blocks would become shattered bone. Of course, if you do not trust me . . ."

"I trust you, Mr. Winch."

"Good. Because now I will give you your man."

"Where will I find him?"

"He will find you," said Mr. Winch. He outlined a plan under which, if Hawley Bardwell followed it faithfully, he would not only have his man but $15,000 as well. And the $15,000 came first.

There were many strange things he did not understand, but to Hawley Bardwell this plan was a delight. Not only would he realize money, as Lynette always said he would if he stayed with Mr. Winch, but he would have his main target, and others, first, to practice on.

Yes, he could kill them if he first practiced the shoulder stroke, and no, there was no chance of his being caught by anyone, except the man who would be his ultimate target.

Bardwell was so excited he wanted to tell Lynette that the place he was going to take the $15,000 from was the very place she worked as a teller. But Mr. Winch had not said he could discuss it, even with his wife, so on the evening of his plan he just told her he was going for a little walk. The way he said it must have warned her, for she said, "Watch your ass there, Hawley," and he responded, "Sure enough," and then he just moseyed out onto the main street of Tenafly, New Jersey, with the shops closing and the police sleepily cruising the dwindling traffic and the crisp wetness of winter upon the New Jersey city waiting for the grace of snow.

As Mr. Winch had explained it, the whole operation was an extension of the stroke. Your protection was your offense.

Down the street he could see lights on in the second story of the Tenafly Trust and Savings Corp. He had two hundred dollars on deposit there, the most he and Lynette could put away on his gym instructor's salary. As she had said so many times, at least they weren't getting in the hole if they could put away even two dollars a week. Lynette always had such good reasoning. Perhaps that was why, of all the wives of his pupils, Mr. Winch seemed to favor her.

Bardwell moved on the street behind the bank. Mr. Winch had warned him not to cut into the narrow alley behind the bank until he was just opposite that building. Police were always checking for burglars in the back of the smaller shops and he should cut his alley time to the minimum. For the police, the bank was the one building that needed the least night supervision. It had the modern time-lock safe, the kind that had put safecrackers out of business. All the money went in there at five every night and was not available to human hands until 8:30 A.M. The illusion of safety was their biggest weakness, Mr. Winch had said.

Bardwell saw the high white concrete ledge of the bank roof rising above the yellow two-story frame house of this residential street just behind the main thoroughfare. He moved quietly down the driveway across a well-mowed yard and over a fence and he was in the alley. He could smell the rich pungent odor from the delicatessen and hear his feet make a small splash as he walked through a puddle left by that afternoon's rain. The bank had three doors, two of them with alarms and bars and wire mesh, for they protected the entrance to the main floor and vault. By financial logic, the third door needed no expensive alarm system for it led only to the executive offices of the president, the senior vice president, and the comptroller. It was secure because there was an effective alarm seal between their offices and the money below, a single inside door.

So Bardwell's hand closed on the key Mr. Winch had given him, and he took it out of his pocket and felt for the lock. He paused and listened. A footstep crushed a tin can. A flashlight sent a terrifying yellow beam down the alley. Bardwell pushed himself into the doorway as he felt the key click. He could disappear into the door but Mr. Winch had told him that at night movement, not objects, attracts attention. So he fought his instinct to put the door between himself and the light, and he kept stillness within him as Mr. Winch had taught. The light continued and the steps came right behind him and he expected a billy stick in his back. It was so close he could hear breathing. But the steps went on also, and when they were a good hundred feet down the alley, Bardwell eased himself into the alcove behind the door and, with a relieving click, shut the door between himself and the outside.

It was dark and he ran his left hand against the wall. He felt a linen-type wallpaper whose ridges were glossy smooth to the fingertips. His left foot bumped a solid vertical. The toe eased up until it was at the first level of the first step and then pushed forward until it hit another vertical. He pressed down on the foot and lifted the other, and slowly he began to climb the back steps. It seemed that the door came on him suddenly, bumping him in the chin.

"Hold it," he heard a man's voice. "Someone's at the door."

"Rubbish," came another man's voice.

"I heard something. I told you I heard something."

"You heard your losing streak. Shut up and deal."

Bardwell pushed open the door and stepped up into the lit office, a plush, beige-carpeted expanse of modern furniture and hanging chrome lights, leather couches, and a shining mahogany table in the shape of a hexagon. Five men looked up from their cards and chips. It was this room's light he had seen from Main Street. It was from this room that he would rob the bankers, despite their time-lock vault downstairs that would be as useless as marbles in a microscope.

"It's Hawley Bardwell," said the senior vice president of Tenafly Trust and Savings. He had his thick-fingered hands over his cards, his sludgy gray eyes glancing from Bardwell to the man on his left, whose cards were tilted forward, an absent-minded exposure obviously caused by Bardwell's entrance.

"Who?" said a flaccid-faced man with crowning silver hair whom Bardwell recognized as the president of Tenafly Trust and Savings. His cards had been lowered beneath the table.

"Lynette Bardwell's husband," said the senior vice president.

"Who?" said the president, adjusting his sleek horn-rim glasses.

"Assistant head teller. Won 'employee of the year' award," said the senior vice president and the president's face squinted in fruitless mental search. The vice president leaned across the table and whispered:

"The blonde with the nice ass, sir."

"Oh. You're the gym teacher they fired for some sort of brutality, Bardwell."

"I was the football coach."

"Oh, well. What do you want? We're having an important meeting, as you can see. Tell me what you want, and after that you can tell me how you got in."

"No meeting," said Bardwell. "It's a card game."

"This is our regular Thursday night meeting, and sometimes we end it with cards," said the president of Tenafly Trust and Savings. "It's also none of your business, Mr. Bardwell. Now, what do you want?"

Hawley Bardwell smiled a delicious smile and he could taste his joy, just looking at the five men. He could no longer resist. He took the closest, whose head was twisted around looking at him and popped him right square in the forehead with the heel of his right hand. The skull whipped back like a giant lead sash had yanked it and the neck snapped like stretched cellophane punctured by a toothpick. The head hit the table, startling the chips in the center with a shock wave.

Before anyone could adjust to the kill and realize

this was something more than a fistfight, Bardwell moved left into the president of Tenafly Trust and Savings, who was raising himself in indignation. Bardwell lowered him with a stroke face center with the fingertips of his flat hand, splitting the jaw like an overstuffed sausage casing. The eyes blinked, the head lowered, and Bardwell flipped the unconscious man across the room and charged into a man backpedaling away, holding his cards in front of his face and wincing. As funny as the fan of cards seemed, they obstructed a solid stroke and Bardwell would not risk his flesh against the celluloid edges. The burly comptroller was across the table swinging at Bardwell from his knees, planted on the pile of chips, and this gave Bardwell his shoulder stroke. The man's left-hand punch was blocked, then his shoulder popped, and Bardwell's right hand drove to the nerves and was back. The comptroller shrieked in pain. Then the senior vice president, who had known Lynette had a nice ass, did a very foolish thing. He went toes centered into the *sanchin dachi* and Bardwell got his second shoulder shot this time with even more help from the blocking elbow. The senior vice president spun as if he were on a cord, and Bardwell moved back into the man, who now cringed in the corner. Bardwell got the cards down with a light kick into the groin and then from a close position, well-centered within himself, used the shoulder stroke skull center. Perhaps it was the wall corners, holding the head square like the inside of a triangle vise, but there was no pop of the neck. Bardwell saw his fingertips surrounded by bloody forehead up to his knuckles. His fingertips felt warm gush, and he knew his nails were in the man's

58

brain. He eased his hand from the moistness and it struck him as odd that it felt like Lynette's vagina. He wiped the reddish gook off on the comptroller's white shirt. Then at his leisure and pleasure, with foot and chairleg, he finished the comptroller, the senior vice president, and the president of Tenafly Trust and Savings, and took from their persons $14,375.

"There's $625 missing," thought Bardwell, but he would not delay longer looking for it. Like almost every employer, these bankers thought their secrets were safe because no one dared mention anything to them. As Mr. Winch had said, "A servant is a person who knows the most about his master and tells him the least." So their secret Thursday night poker game was a secret just to them. Others knew, and men as brilliant as Mr. Winch could find out, about bankers who knew most of all that a check wasn't nearly as good as cash, especially in a gambling game. Bankers who wouldn't trust their colleagues for a temporary loan, bankers who every Thursday night brought $3,000 apiece to a poker game and shielded the game from the street with only their minds, not even bothering to draw drapes. Bankers who thought there was nothing safer than a bank. Dead men.

That night, when Lynette lusted, Hawley Bardwell turned away from her in the bed. How could he tell her he had already been totally satisfied that evening, and just sex with a woman would be a pale letdown, something akin to masturbating after spending a weekend with a sexy movie star.

He not only had what he wanted, but, as Mr. Winch said, he would have more. It was all to get the man he wanted. His target.

When the target was notified of what the press called "the horror at the bank," he thought the call from upstairs was notification that Chiun was returning from Sinanju, or had changed his mind about going.

"No, Remo," said Smith. "Sub left on schedule. He's gone. But I would suggest you read carefully a very interesting story out of Tenafly, New Jersey. I think we've been given a break."

"Why?"

"You don't know what happened in Tenafly? It's the biggest story in the country today. It has all the gruesome and irrelevant facts that the press loves. But there's something in it for us, too. I'm surprised you didn't catch it on a newsstand."

"I haven't been out today."

"It was in yesterday's papers, too. I thought you would be in Tenafly by now."

"Wasn't out yesterday either," said Remo. "Or the day before."

"Well, I think you should get out now and look at the story. Particularly the way the men died."

"Yeah. Right. Right away," said Remo. He hung up and watched the light on the taping machine that indicated Chiun's programs were being recorded for his return. The machine would turn off automatically by three-thirty P.M. that afternoon, but Remo watched the light anyway for the whole afternoon. By four P.M. he had a sock on and by seven P.M. he had the other sock on, and by ten o'clock he was in his shorts with trousers, and by the time it was all put together with turtleneck sweater and tan loafers, it was eleven-thirty P.M., so Remo postponed the trip until the next morning when, wearing the clothes he had slept in, he left the motel at four-thirty A.M. because he couldn't sleep anymore.

The clerk at the motel outside Raleigh-Durham Airport asked where Remo's friend was because everyone had taken a liking to him even though the old Oriental didn't go out much, and Remo answered:

"I don't need him and I don't even miss him."

"Oh sure, sure," said the clerk. "Just asking if he was going to come back, sort of."

"I couldn't care less," said Remo.

"Sure," said the clerk.

"You got newspapers here?"

"Just yesterday's."

"Fine," said Remo.

"When will you be back?"

"Couple of days or so. Don't touch my television."

"Sure. What should I do if the old fella comes back while you're gone?"

"He won't," said Remo, and he heard his voice crack. On the plane, which landed at Newark, he read about the "the horror at the bank."

He took a taxi to Tenafly, a rather long and expensive trip, and when he got to the bank there appeared to be no police lines.

"In back," said a passerby. "It happened up there on the second floor, but everyone is in the back."

In the alley behind the bank, Remo found a police cordon and a small crowd hanging around in front of it. He checked his wallet, leafed through cards identifying him as an FBI man, Treasury agent, representative of the Food and Drug Administration, and a freelance magazine writer. Unlike other cover identifications, every one of these cards were real. There was a listing in every one of these organizations for a man named Remo Pelham or Remo Bednick or Remo Dalton or Remo Slote. The organizations never saw him because he was always on special assignment, but he would always be vouched for if someone checked.

"Pinnacle Magazine," said Remo, flashing the card to a patrolman at the cordon. "Who's in charge?"

It was a dull twenty-five minutes as he listened to the deputy chief of police, who three times repeated the spelling of his own name, explain the gruesome five-man murder. The deputy chief wasn't sure if the motive was robbery because $625 in cash was found in the center of the table under a pile of chips. But it could have been robbery because everyone knew the five bankers always brought $3,000 apiece to their regular Thursday night poker game. It was a thing people didn't talk about much. There were, the deputy chief explained, at least three instruments used in the mass murder. He personally believed one of the instruments was a blunted spear. A chair leg was another of them. They couldn't get prints from the chair yet but don't write that, said the deputy chief.

"The horror of men's minds always astounds me," said the deputy chief and asked Remo if he wanted an eight by ten glossy of the deputy chief taken upon his promotion to that rank.

"You say these guys were hit in the head, shoulders, and chest?"

"Right. One guy's skull was cracked clean through. That's where I got my blunted spear theory. You might want to call this the blunted spear murder case. Did you get my name correctly? I don't see you taking notes." The chief looked at the crowd on the other

62

side of the police lines and waved. "Hi, Hawley, c'mon over," he shouted with a wave, and in a lower voice said to Remo: "Used to be our football coach. Good one, too. Fired him because he wanted to make winners out of spoiled brats. You know, New Yorkers coming over here. Afraid their little Sammy's going to get his big beak broken . . . don't quote me . . . well, hello, Hawley."

And the deputy chief introduced Remo to the man, who stood a good four inches above Remo, a broad-shouldered, well-muscled man whose walk aroused Remo's curiosity. It had a certain familiar balance, not quite the way Remo or Chiun walked, but a hint of similar principles.

"This is Hawley Bardwell. Wife works in the bank and he's worried about her safety. Comes here every day since the incident. Hawley, this is Remo Slote. He's a magazine writer."

Bardwell offered his big hand to shake and Remo noticed the man's eyes focus on his wrists. It was a strong handshake and Remo wiggled out of it by collapsing his palm and thrusting his hand into his pocket.

"You don't have to worry, Hawley. Whoever did it is a thousand miles away by now," said the deputy chief.

"I guess you're right," said Bardwell. He was smiling.

"Can I see the bodies?" asked Remo.

"Oh, two were buried right away. Religious thing, you know. The other three are still at the funeral homes. Their burial's tomorrow."

"I'd like to see the bodies."

63

"Well, that's sort of delicate. The families are having closed coffin funerals. But we have pictures back at headquarters."

"Not as good as the bodies," said Remo.

"I'm a close friend of one of the families," said Bardwell. "Maybe I can help."

"I didn't know that," said the deputy chief.

"Yeah," said Bardwell. "That is, before everyone started forgetting they knew me when I was fired."

"I always supported you, Hawley. I thought you did wonders with what you had. Always supported you."

"Not publicly," said Bardwell.

"Well, not exactly out in the open. I've got my job."

"Yeah," said Bardwell. "C'mon, Mr. Slote," he said to Remo. "I'll show you the bodies that are still above ground."

"You shouldn't take it so hard, Hawley. You'll get another job," said the deputy chief.

"I expect so," said Bardwell. All the way to McAlpin's Funeral Home, he explained to Remo how it must have been a dozen men who killed the bankers, because of the terrible injuries.

"Uh huh," agreed Remo.

McAlpin's was a dark-carpeted, quiet private house, transformed with some neat carpentry into a funeral home.

"They'll be waking tonight. But we can get a good look now because no one's here in the afternoon," said Bardwell.

"I thought you knew the family."

"That's just something I told the chief. He's got balls of tapioca."

The coffin was white ash, polished to a high gloss, and Remo wondered at all the fine furniture that was made just to be planted with an occupant who couldn't care less. The room smelled of Pineclear air freshener, and the two walked up the aisle of dark folding chairs. Bardwell opened the coffin. A man's skull was waxed down the middle with skin colored wax powdered over. Remo pressed down on the wax to see how wide the cavity. His thumb collected powder and he rubbed it away with a forefinger.

"They had to scoop out some of the brains, I hear, just to get the head closed again," said Bardwell. Remo saw perspiration form on his forehead. Saliva collected in a small pool at a corner of his lips.

"I heard there were some people with their shoulders hurt," said Remo. "That's what the papers said. That they were immobilized first at the shoulder and then killed."

"Yeah," said Bardwell in a heavy breathy gasp. "Whadddya think of that head, huh? Isn't that the worst thing you've ever seen? Huh?"

"No," said Remo. "The guy should have used a gun instead of his hands. If he's going to use his hands that way, he might as well use something wild as a gun."

"What wild?"

"You don't need that much in the central forehead. The hand must have gone into it up to the knuckles. You only need a break and a minimum of pressure inside the brain for an instant kill. Sloppy. I bet it was some karate idiot on a spree."

"But don't you think it's fantastic that somebody with a bare hand could do that? Don't ya? Huh? Don't ya?" said Bardwell.

"Inferior," said Remo and he noticed Bardwell smiling and centralizing his balance, and then because he had been trained to, Remo did something wrong because his body did something right. Bardwell's right hand shot out at Remo and Remo took it, but in doing so, he felt a small direct pressure on his left shoulder and Bardwell's hand kept going through and into the shoulder. An insane stroke. A stroke of such incredible, suicidal stupidity that Remo had never seen it before. And what made it so insane was that the power and accuracy required training, but no one would ever train for something like that. It was suicide against anyone with a serious level of competence.

Bardwell's right hand was into Remo's shoulder while at the same time his face, whole head, throat, and heart were open as a gift to Remo's right hand or right leg. It was a here-I-am-kill-me thrust, and Remo's right hand had but a half a foot to go to catch Bardwell's throat, splitting the thorax and driving pieces of it back into the vertebrae. Bardwell had set himself up for his own death just to get in a cheapie shoulder shot. Remo felt the pain in the left shoulder and wiggled the fingers of his left hand. He could still do that. But the arm would raise only slightly.

Bardwell could raise nothing. He lay at the foot of the coffin, his tongue lounging out of his mouth, forced out of his jaw by the pressure from the throat.

"Shit," said Remo. He had found the man who could talk about the death of William Ashley, and he had killed him because he had reacted automatically. It was almost as if the man had been set up so Remo would have to kill him. Now Remo had not only stifled his possible explanation of why Smitty's man was killed, but he also had a body to get rid of. He worked with his right hand, letting his painful left shoulder hang limp.

Underneath the comptroller with the patched-up forehead, underneath the white silk and the styrofoam red rosary, was bedding, the final support for a body that needed no support. Remo pushed back the white ash lid and with his right hand grabbed the belt of the corpse and deposited it on the other side of the lid. He paused and listened. No movement. No one was coming. He whistled a moving tune he had heard Aretha Franklin sing, remembering only the "needya, baby, baby, needya, baby."

He took the fine seam out of the silk covering at the bottom of the coffin and found cheap cardboard supports. He ripped the cardboard down to bare unfinished wood and placed it in a pile at his feet. His one hand worked like a flashing blade as he picked up the rolling beat of the song and lost the tune so totally he would never find it again.

He grabbed a handful of Bardwell's muscled stomach and hoisted the corpse up into the bare bottom of the coffin. He flattened Bardwell for a better fit, eliminating the bumps of the chest and head without breaking skin. Then, crushing the cardboard at his feet, he reconstructed the well sides around Bardwell and covered it again with the white silk, carefully tucking in the edges.

"Perfect almost," muttered Remo. "Needya, baby, baby."

He took the comptroller of the Tenafly Savings and Trust Company off the lid and put him gently into his final resting place and stepped back to examine his work.

"Shit." The comptroller was three inches too high. Maybe he could get an inch and a half off him and this time he cracked the corpse's spinal column, put a hairline midchest, and pressed down on the groin area, for the comptroller had been well padded in the posterior. Where Bardwell was slim, the comptroller was fat and vice versa. So it worked.

Remo stepped back again.

"Nice fit," he said. Of course, by the time the wake became active, with people coming by to pay last respects, the release of Bardwell's sphincter muscles might cause an unnerving smell, but for now, a nice job. Remo heard someone and quickly touched up the powder on the comptroller's cold face.

"Baby, baby, needya, baby," sung Remo and from behind him a whiny voice called out:

"You there. What are you doing with the deceased?"

Remo turned and saw a man in black suit, white shirt, and black tie with a very pale face, pale because he used the same powder on himself as he had used on the comptroller.

"Just a friend of the deceased."

"The wake's tonight. I know who you are. I know your kind. If you've played with that man's privates . . ."

"What?" said Remo.

"Sick," said the man. "You're sick. Sick. Sick."

"I was just saying goodbye to a friend."

"I bet, sicko. I know your kind. Hang around funeral homes trying to get jobs but you'll never get one in mine. You know why? You're sick is why. That's why."

"If you say so," said Remo.

"Glad I caught you before you could get to anything."

"Thank you," said Remo, taking it as a compliment for his work.

At the bank he saw the deputy chief again, who introduced him to the head teller, who pointed out Lynette Bardwell. She had a strong, elegant face with a faint almond shaping to her gray eyes and neat, bouncy blonde hair, streaked with just the right touch of darker blonde. Her lips were full and moist and she carried herself with a calmness. Even under the formal stiff white blouse and tweed skirt, Remo could sense the beauty of her body. He wondered what she had seen in Bardwell.

He waited until the bank was closed to customers and then, with the head teller's permission, took her into one of the private rooms where customers examined safe deposit boxes.

"Why do you want to interview me?" asked Lynette. She was only in her early twenties, yet she seemed unflustered by the interview.

"Because your husband is the man who slaughtered those bankers upstairs."

Lynette Bardwell lit a filter tip cigarette and exhaled.

"I know that," she said. "What do you want?"

"I'm interested in his friends, who might have taught him what he knew about handling himself in a fight."

"And just who are you?"

"I'm the man your husband confessed to."

"That dumb bastard," said Lynette, and her composure disappeared as she surrendered to teary sobs. "That dumb bastard."

CHAPTER FIVE

As he watched her weep, Remo realized he had overestimated Lynette Bardwell's toughness. He had listened to that nasal bray that New Jersey women called human speech, and had been fooled by it. Lynette Bardwell was just a woman, soft and yielding. He decided not to tell her that her husband was dead.

Lynette blotted her eyes with a tissue and looked up. "If you want to talk all night, you've got to buy me a sandwich."

"Don't you think Hawley will mind?" asked Remo, not really caring. For Hawley Bardwell to mind would involve his raising himself from the dead, getting past one body, and out of a sealed coffin. Remo wasn't worried.

"Suppose he does?"

"He's a pretty fast guy with his hands, I suppose. He might light into you pretty hard."

"Hah. That'll be the day," said Lynette. "Look, big magazine writer, are you on an expense account or not?"

"Yes."

"Then no sandwich. Dinner. A real dinner."

Lynette Bardwell's idea of a real dinner was a cinder block structure outside the city that had changed from diner to restaurant by adding wood paneling, tables instead of booths, and turning down the lights. No one apparently had bothered to tell the chef of the

71

change in status because the menu was still built upon one-plate meals, most of them seeming to specialize in chopped meat.

Lynette ordered salad—"it's nice and crisp here all the time"—to which Remo did not comment, contenting himself instead with the thought that so was birchbark. She wanted Thousand Island dressing, sirloin steak rare, baked potato with cheese mixed in, asparagus tips with hollandaise sauce, and a Tom Collins in a tall glass to start everything off.

Remo asked for a glass of water to start things off, and rice, if the cook had long-grained wild rice, with no seasoning, no salt, no pepper, no monosodium glutamate, and if they did not have long-grained wild rice, he would settle for just the water.

Which he did, because the chef had never heard of wild rice and if it was made by Minute Rice he would have known about it. The waitress snapped her gum as she told Remo this and delivered the water. He sipped it. It was good to be back home in New Jersey where the water contained trace elements of every one of the known elements, including macadam.

Lynette sipped at her Tom Collins, carefully replacing it on the paper napkin between sips, and asked Remo suddenly:

"What's wrong with your shoulder?"

"Why?"

"It looks like you're holding it funny," she said. "Like it's hurting."

"Touch of arthritis," said Remo, who thought he had been disguising the immobility of his left arm. "Where did Hawley learn his karate?"

72

"Oh, he's been at it for years. There are places in Jersey City that he goes to."

"You know the name of them?" asked Remo, putting the water aside for when he might really want it, like after a thirty-day trek in the Sahara.

"Not really. I don't pay any attention to that. I don't know what kick some men get out of hopping around in pajamas."

"You prefer men hopping around without pajamas?"

Lynette giggled. "Well, maybe not hopping," she said. She raised the glass to her mouth and looked over the top of it at Remo. "What makes you think Hawley killed those bankers?"

"He told me," said Remo.

"Just like that? He told you? 'I killed the bankers and stole their money?'"

"Almost," Remo said. "He kind of bragged about the different strokes used on them. He talked too much about it not to have done it."

"Did you tell him you knew?"

"Yes."

"And then what?"

"He said he was going on a trip."

"Somehow I don't believe you," she said. "If Hawley knew you knew, then I think he would have smacked you around, too."

"Maybe he was afraid of me. Maybe I look like another guy who hops around wearing pajamas."

Lynette shook her head. "No, no. Definitely not. You're not the pajama type."

"How did you know he did the killings?" asked Remo.

"He told me." Remo waited for her to fill in the blanks, but she said nothing more.

"Have another drink," said Remo.

Lynette Bardwell did. And another. And another. That was before the steak (well done and stringy), the baked potato (burned to a crisp), and the asparagus tips (not tips but spears).

She did not seem to mind. She ate doggedly through it, reveling in the dim lights and the canned music by two hundred and two violins, and she had yet another drink and leaned on Remo heavily as she lurched with him toward her car.

"Suppose Hawley's home?" said Remo. "Maybe I should stop near your house and you can drive home yourself?"

"He won't be," she said with some confidence. "Home, James."

She snored a little bit. She woke up near her house, sat upright, and snapped her fingers. "I just remembered," she said thickly.

"What?"

"There's a guy Hawley practices with. Another karate freak."

"What's his name?"

"Fred Westerly."

"Where do I find him? I'd like to know more about all this karate stuff."

"He's a cop. I remember now. A policeman. A lieutenant or something. I think he's in the training school. Hawley mentioned him once. Yeah. Jersey City. He trains cops in Jersey City."

"Fred Westerly, huh?"

"Thass right," Lynette said, and her head dropped

onto Remo's shoulder and she was asleep again.

Getting out of the car, she lurched heavily against Remo's left shoulder, forcing him to grit his teeth against the explosions of pain that sounded inside his skull. Biting hard on his lip, he sleepwalked her upstairs to the bedroom in the Bardwell's tiny frame Cape Cod on the edge of town.

She put up no resistance as Remo undressed her and put her under the covers. Before he left, Remo did a thing to the nerves under her left armpit and whispered in her ear, "Dream of me. I'm going to be back."

She smiled in her sleep.

As he walked away from the house, Remo saw a small light click on in the upstairs bathroom.

CHAPTER SIX

Captain Lee Enright Leahy of the U.S. Submarine *Darter* had made this trip before. Five times in five years and each time he understood it less. Because of the destination, he couldn't embark from Japan. Russia and North Korea got copy on any ships leaving through the Sea of Japan and especially submarines, and anyone making port at Taiwan or the Ryukyu Islands might as well forget it. You could add China, too. So much for normal secrecy for normal trips.

For this trip, you had to start evasive action at San Diego, spreading the word you were heading for Australia, letting crew wives know their husband's next port was Darwin. You crossed the Pacific practically at flank speed, entering the East China Sea submerged between Miyako and Naha Islands. Then you headed north into the East China Sea, risked the China coast within a hundred miles of Shanghai, and kept on the China side as you entered the Yellow Sea, because if the Chinese did get copy on you, there would be a delay, hopefully, before they would inform North Korea. At latitude thirty-eight and longitude one twenty-four, you veered north by northeast into the West Korean Bay and then, in that infernal joint where North Korea and Communist China meet, you let out a team of SEALS (Sea Air Land) boys, the descendants of frogmen, Rangers, OSS, and every other whacko group that the military was forced to use on missions on which they would not send the sane.

And all this to deliver a tiny purse of gold to an old woman who would meet them on the coast, just outside the village of Sinanju, at three A.M. every November 12.

What puzzled Captain Leahy was that the bag contained less than $10,000 in gold, and it cost hundreds of thousands of dollars to deliver and risked millions plus an international incident. He had wondered why the CIA (he was sure it was the CIA) couldn't find a safer and cheaper contact route, or at least deliver three years' gold at once, thus eliminating two risky trips.

So when the *Darter* turned north into the East China Sea, only to surface later that evening, Captain Leahy thought he would visit with the passenger. This time they had a passenger who was not only bringing the gold, but clumsy bolts of cloth, boxes of jewels, a clumsily framed, autographed picture of an insignificant soap opera actor, and three outsized lacquered trunks. How they were ever going to fit into the rubber rafts, he didn't know. But he was grateful that he had gotten away with refusing to surface and carry electronic gear that would pick up, of all things, television shows that some idiot in the Pentagon was thinking of beaming to the Pacific just for the *Darter*.

At that suggestion, Leahy had popped his apple.

"Dammit. There are safer and saner ways to transmit information than through television," he had said.

"It's not exactly information," said the admiral who coordinated CIA-Navy relations.

"Well, what is it?"

77

"Television shows."

"You mean newscasts or something?"

"Not exactly. The shows listed are, minus commercials, twenty-one minutes and fifteen seconds of *As the Planet Revolves,* thirteen minutes and ten seconds, minus commercials of *The Young and the Raw,* twenty-four minutes and forty-five seconds, minus commercials, *The Edge of Life.* Total transmission time would be under an hour."

"I'm supposed to surface between China and North Korea, with Russia looking on, to pick up soap operas? What's happened to you people?"

"We got the commercials knocked out," said the admiral. "With commercials, it would go an hour and fifteen minutes."

"What is this thing anyhow?" asked Captain Leahy.

"We're not in the habit of letting everyone be privy to the broader picture, Captain."

"Is anyone privy to the broader picture?"

"Well, frankly, Captain, I don't know either. This one's so supersecret I'm not even totally sure it's CIA. Do you want me to put down an absolute 'no' on the surfacing for television shows?"

"Like slightly," said Captain Leahy.

"You're refusing the mission if you have to surface for the shows?"

"I am refusing."

"Can't say as I blame you. Let me see if we can get the shows bumped."

By sailing time, the admiral was beaming triumph. "I went to the wire and we won," he said. He was wearing civilian clothes and standing on the conning tower of the *Darter*. "You're down to three steamer trunks in the rubber rafts."

"You ever try to paddle a steamer trunk in a rubber raft in the West Korea Bay in November?"

"You don't have to succeed," said the admiral with a broad wink. "All you've got to do is try. Good luck, Lee."

"Thank you, sir," said Captain Leahy. Now he remembered the admiral's wink as he passed the steamer trunks lashed to the bulkhead and knocked on the door of the passenger's compartment.

"It's Captain Leahy."

"Yes," came the squeaky voice.

"I want you to know we're entering the Yellow Sea," said Captain Leahy.

"Then you are not lost. Is that what you are telling me?"

"Well, not exactly. I wanted to talk to you about debarkation."

"Are we at Sinanju?"

"No. The Yellow Sea. I told you."

"Then there is no need to discuss whatever-it-is-you-said."

"Well, your trunks are sort of heavy and I'm not sure the SEALS can paddle them in."

"Oh, how typical white," came the voice from inside the compartment. "You have the only ships that cannot carry things."

"We could carry in a whole city if we had to, but not into old Kim Il Sung's North Korea. The premier is not one of our most ardent admirers."

"Why should he be when you are such a defiler of the arts? Do not deny it. It was you who refused to

79

give an old man the simple pleasure of a daytime drama."

"Sir, we might all have gotten ourselves blown out of the water if we surfaced to pick up those television shows. I refused for your own good. Would you want to be captured by the Chinese?"

"Captured?"

"Yes. You know, taken prisoner. Thrown in a dungeon."

"The hands that can do that have yet to be put on human wrists. Away, you imitation sailor."

"Sir, sir . . ." But there was no answer and the passenger did not come up on deck or respond to knocks until the *USS Darter* finally surfaced off the coast of Sinanju. All the men were bundled in cold weather gear, their eyes peering out of cold weather masks; the decks were icy and the wind was tossing ice spears at their backs.

"Here he is," said one of the sailors, and the deck crew stared in disbelief, for a frail old man, barely tall enough to see over the bridge, climbed down to the deck in only a dark gray kimono whipped by the China winds, his wisps of beard fluttering, his head uncovered, his hands in repose beneath the kimono.

"Sir, sir," shouted the captain. "The SEALS can't get your trunks into the rubber raft. They won't fit and even if they did, in this sea, you'd capsize."

"Do you think the Master of Sinanju would entrust his treasures to an imitation sailor, working for an imitation Navy? Bring the trunks to the deck and lash them together, end to end like a train. You have seen trains, have you not?"

80

And thus it was done upon the boat of the white men with the round eyes, and the three trunks of the Master of Sinanju that would float were bound together. For the Master had rightly thought to bring only those trunks that could sustain themselves, knowing this in all clarity: A sailor who cannot haul simple baggage for something as precious as a drama of beauty and truth is a sailor to whom one could not entrust the wealth of a village.

And wrapped in skins and clothes of nylon, their tender faces covered from the home winds that were strange to them, the white sailors lowered the trunks that had been carved and welded by Park Yee, the carpenter, the trunks which had lasted in the new land discovered by the grandfather of Chiun in the year of the dog—the year before the good czar sold the bridge of the North Peninsula called Alaska to the same Americans that Yui, the grandfather of Chiun, had discovered.

And the trunks in the home sea floated behind the flimsy yellow boats of the white men. Now, know it that all the white men were not white in color. Some were black and some were brown and some even yellow. Yet their minds had been destroyed by whiteness so that their souls were white.

Chiun, the Master of Sinanju, himself rode the last boat near the trunks, which were tribute for his people. And lo, upon the darkened shore, he saw standing a beautiful young maiden, upon the rocks above the large cove. But alas, she was alone.

"Ever see such a pig?" asked a bosun's mate, nodding toward the fat-faced Korean woman squatting on the ugly outcropping of rock.

81

"Yeah. In a zoo," said the other paddler.

"At least she wears heavy clothes. The old gook must have antifreeze for blood. This wind'd numb a yak."

The radio on the raft crackled with a message from the sub, surfaced six hundred yards offshore. A column of lights was approaching from Sinanju. Heavy vehicles. Possibly tanks.

The squad leader of the SEALS informed his passenger of approaching trouble. "You can return to the sub with us. But we have to go now. Right now."

"I am home," Chiun said to the young man.

"That means you're staying?"

"I will not flee."

"Okay, fella. It's your ass."

Chiun smiled and watched the frightened men scramble back into their rafts and paddle back toward the ship that bobbed on the waters of the bay. The girl climbed down from the rocks, approached, and bowed deeply. Her words were like music to Chiun, the words of his childhood and of games in which he had learned the secrets of the body and mind and of the forces of the universe. The language of home was sweet.

"Hail, Master of Sinanju, who sustains the village and keeps the code faithfully, leader of the House of Sinanju. Our hearts cry a thousand greetings of love and adoration. Joyous are we upon the return of him who throttles the universe."

"Graciously throttles the universe," corrected Chiun.

"Graciously throttles the universe," repeated the girl, who had been practicing all week and had worried only about "adoration," because that was the word she had forgotten most. "Graciously throttles the universe."

"Why are you alone, child?"

"It is not permitted anymore to practice the old ways."

"Who does not permit?"

"The People's Democratic Republic."

"The whores in Pyongyang?" asked Chiun.

"We are not allowed to call the government that any more."

"And why do you venture here, child?"

"I am the granddaughter of the carpenter by the bay. We are the last family who believes in the old ways."

"My cousins and my wife's cousins and my wife's brothers and their cousins, what of them?"

"They are of the new way. Your wife is long since gone."

In the way the girl said this, Chiun knew there was something she was hiding that was painful.

"I knew of my wife's death," said Chiun. "But there is something else. What is it?"

"She denounced the House of Sinanju, Master."

Chiun smiled. "Such is the way of her family. Such always was her nature. Do not weep, my child. For in all the universe, there never was a harder heart nor more base family."

"The People's Government forced her," said the girl.

"No," said Chiun. "They could not force what was not there. Her family was always jealous of the House of Sinanju and she came to it with bitterness. And she

83

led me to the great mistake." Chiun's voice broke on the last two words as he remembered how he had taken in the son of his brother, at his wife's continual urging, and how that son of his brother had left the village to use the secrets of Sinanju to gain power and wealth. And such was the disgrace to Chiun that Chiun, whose name had been Nuihc, reversed the sounds and became Chiun, leaving the old name of Nuihc for disgrace. And the disgrace had sent Chiun forth from the village to sustain it by his labors and talents, at a time when he should have enjoyed the golden years of his life in comfort and respect.

"She said, O Master, that you had taken a white to teach. But my grandfather said, no, that would be the debasement typical of your nephew and your wife's family."

Above the dark ridge, Chiun saw a procession of lights making their way to the cove.

"That was a courageous thing for your grandfather to say. I hope the tribute sent to the village has softened the hearts of some toward me."

"We never got the gold, O Master. It went to the People's Party. They were here this year also to collect it, but when the collectors saw that you came yourself they ran back to the village for help. I alone stayed, because I have learned this speech every time this year on the possible occasion of your return."

"You held to the old ways with no payment?" asked Chiun.

"Yes, Master of Sinanju. For without you, we are just another poor village. But with the tradition of your house, we are the home of the Masters of Sinanju and yea, though the world spins through chaos or glory, Sinanju is something because of you and your ancestors. This I have been taught. I am sorry I forgot 'graciously.'"

Hearing this, Chiun wept and brought the girl to his bosom.

"Know you now, Child, all you and your family have suffered will be but memories. Your family shall know glory. This I promise you with my life. The sun of this day shall not set without your exaltation. Be despised in the village no longer. For among all the people, you alone are pure and good."

And by way of a joke to ease the burden of the girl's heart, Chiun noted that usually "adoration" was forgotten.

And now the people of the village were upon them, and the man called Comrade Captain, who had been a fisherman, accosted Chiun, the Master of Sinanju, standing before his tribute in the cove. Surrounded by men and the armaments of war, Comrade Captain showed bravery.

"In the name of the people of Sinanju and for the People's Democratic Republic of Korea, I claim the tribute."

And behind the captain, people yelled and cheered and applauded and some raised guns above their heads and others banged on a large tank which they had brought with them to show their new power.

"If you claim it," said Chiun, "then who among you will lay hand on it? Who will be first?"

"We will all do it at one time."

And the Master of Sinanju smiled and said: "You think you will all do it at one time. But one hand will be the first and I will see that hand and then that hand will move no more."

"We are many and you are but one," said Comrade Captain.

"Hear you this. Cow dung is many but the cow is few, and who does not trample dung with contempt. This I feel for you. Yea, though the shores were covered with you, I would but tread distastefully through you. Only one among you is worthy. This child."

And they jeered the Master of Sinanju and cursed the granddaughter of the carpenter and called her all manner of unclean things. And Comrade Captain said unto the people of Sinanju, "Let us take his tribute for we are many and he is but one."

And they rushed forward with a joyous shout, but at the trunks which had floated in along with the Master, no hand moved to touch, for none wanted to be first. And the people were still. Then the captain said, "I will be first. And should I fall then all will descend on you."

And as he touched the first trunk of tribute, Chiun, the Master of Sinanju, said to the people he would also see who would be first to lay hand upon the Master and that person would perish.

And with that, he slew the captain before the trunks, and Comrade Captain was still in death, and the people moved not. Then an old woman, from north of the village where the tradesmen lived, said they had more power than Chiun, the Master of Sinanju. They had a tank which was all powerful. And the people made way for the trunk, all but the granddaughter of the carpenter, who had been reviled. She alone stood with the Master of Sinanju.

But when the tank was upon the Master of Sinanju, his great hands moved with their awesome skill and

86

one tread popped and then the other so that the tank was mired with its own weight and could not move, like a man numbed by wine.

And upon this helpless tank climbed Chiun and sealed the top hatch. And with such awesome leverage that no man had, he made the turret still and cracked from its front the guns that could kill many.

Now beneath tanks were other hatches, but this tank had settled into wet sand and the hatches could not open.

"Those in here I leave for the tide," said the Master of Sinanju, and there was moaning and crying from within the tank. For these soldiers, although they came from Pyongyang, knew the tide would soon be upon them and would drown them, and they begged for mercy.

But Chiun would hear none of it, and he called the people close around him and he said to them: "But for this child, none of you would see another day. You have made light of the tribute and desecrated the name of the House of Sinanju in its own village."

But the child begged that Chiun not be harsh with the people for they were in fear of the whore city Pyongyang and the evil ones who lived along the Yalu and the corrupt in the large cities like Hamhung where people wrote things on paper for common folk to perform. She begged him that he share the tribute with all, and the Master of Sinanju told her that even though none was worthy, they would share because she asked. And those inside the tank asked if they too could be spared.

But Chiun would hear none of it, and he called for them anyhow. The old woman from the tradesmen's quarters said if it were not for the evil ones in

Pyongyang they would have greeted the Master properly in the first place. So it was agreed to leave them.

The granddaughter of the carpenter said those inside the tank were doing what they were told because of the same fear and that they should be allowed mercy also, but Chiun said "Pyongyang is Pyongyang and Sinanju is Sinanju."

All knew he meant that those in the tank did not matter, and upon reflection the granddaughter agreed that the Master of Sinanju was right. They were from Pyongyang.

So with many praises, the villagers carried the trunks back to the village with the girl high among them. And many said they had always loved her but were afraid of Pyongyang, and many offered marriage to her and placed her with great honor. All this before the sun rose.

There was great rejoicing in the village, but the Master of Sinanju showed no joy. For he remembered the white man, dead of the many blows of contempt, and he knew a great battle was yet to come in Sinanju, and the man who had to win it was another white man.

© Lorillard 1975

Come for the filter...

A PRODUCT OF *Lorillard*

KENT

WITH
THE FAMOUS MICRONITE FILTER

DELUXE LENGTH

© Lorillard 1975

...you'll stay for the taste.

A lot of good taste that comes easy through the Micronite filter.

18 mg. "tar," 1.2 mg. nicotine av. per cigarette, FTC Report Oct. '74.

CHAPTER SEVEN

"No, no, no!"

The two men facing each other on the tumbling mats froze in place.

"You two shits are hopeless," bellowed the man who walked onto the mats between them. He was a burly man with lumps of muscle for shoulders and the bristly mustache of a British sergeant major. He wore a white karate uniform with a black sash that was slung low and tied down in the area of his groin. He raised his hand to his face and the overhead lights glinted off his manicured fingernails.

"This isn't a frigging dance," he yelled again. "You, Needham . . . you're supposed to be killing this man. Trying to choke him. You ain't squeezing with enough power to wrinkle a grape."

He turned around. "And you, Foster. He's supposed to be a killer and you're supposed to take him out. Fast. Christ help the public if you two ever get out on the street."

Needham, a tall thin man with a wiry brush-cut who looked like an upside-down broom, grimaced at the back of Lieutenant Fred Wetherby. He thought he had been squeezing hard enough to hurt. Foster, an athletically muscled black man, said nothing, but let his eyes bespeak his contempt for the mustached police lieutenant. A dozen police recruits, sitting on the floor around the mats waiting their turn to wrestle, saw the look. So did Lieutenant Wetherby, who turned back to Needham.

"Needham. Step forward."

The thin man moved forward, his slowness betraying his unsureness.

"Now try it on me," Wetherby said. Needham put his two hands up to Wetherby's thick sloping neck. As he was doing it, he decided that perhaps he was not really cut out to be a policeman. He was not happy with hand-to-hand combat.

He could not get his hands around Wetherby's neck, but he squeezed as hard as he could, keeping his muscles tensed for the throw he knew was coming.

"Squeeze, goddammit," Wetherby roared. "You don't have no more strength than a girl. Or a pansy."

Needham clenched the throat tightly. His thumbs found Wetherby's Adam's apple. He pressed in with his thumbs in a flash of anger. He felt a numbing blast hit his right forearm. He tried to keep squeezing but his fingers lost control. He knew that his right hand was slipping loose. He felt a duplicate of the first blow hit the inside of his left forearm. He willed himself to keep squeezing. Keep squeezing this bastard. Rip his throat out. He tried, but the left hand, too, slid loose, and then he felt a sharp pain in the pit of his stomach. He had forgotten, in his anger, to keep those muscles tense to absorb the impact of the blow, and then he felt himself going over Wetherby's back and he hit hard onto the mat. Over his head he saw Wetherby's face, his long thin lips pulled tight in a grimace of hatred, and he saw Wetherby's foot raise up over his head and then come slamming down toward his nose. It was going to hit his nose. He knew it. It was going to mash his face in and make him bleed and shatter and blast his nose bones into his nasal passages.

Needham screamed.

The callused bare heel of the big man touched his nose.

And stopped.

Needham could see the spaces between Wetherby's toes, only a few inches from his eyes. He could see the hard, tanned calluses on the bottom of the lieutenant's foot.

Wetherby stood still a moment, the ball of his foot still touching Needham's nose, and then his thin lips opened and his widely spaced teeth showed in a smile, and he took a deep breath. "Okay, Needham," he said. "You were squeezing hard that time but you forgot to fall right. Remember, roll and slap your arms to spread the impact out."

He nodded. "Okay. Off the mat." Needham, who would realize only later that his fears about being killed in front of a class of fellow police recruits were irrational and groundless, rolled over and moved, sorely stiff, off the mat.

Wetherby turned back toward Foster who had watched the action with a fixed grin.

"Now that's the way to do it," Wetherby said. "No pattycake. Break the hold, throw the man and stomp. Is any of this seeping in through that concrete barrier you call a skull?"

His eyes met Foster's and he saw a glint of anger in the black man's. Wetherby did not bother to show any emotion. He did not like blacks; he thought they destroyed any police force they served on; he especially disliked them when they were cocky as Foster was.

"Do you think you can do it now?" Wetherby asked.

"Oh, I can do it, Lieutenant," said Foster. "Don't you worry about it."

"I never worry."

Foster stepped forward into the center of the mat.

"Ready?" asked Wetherby.

The black recruit bounced up and down in place, light athlete's movements to distribute his weight evenly and make sure his balance was proper.

"Okay," he said. "Go on ... sir," he added in a verbal sneer.

Wetherby slowly raised his hairy thick arms and took a light grip on Foster's slick brown neck.

"Go!" he shouted and squeezed.

Foster felt the sudden shock of pressure on his throat. He felt the pain of thumbs pressing into his Adam's Apple. He did as he had been taught.

He curled his left hand into a fist and punched upward toward the ceiling, between Wetherby's two arms, then slammed his left arm outward. The force of the blow was supposed to force the strangler's right arm to let loose. But, instead of the crash of bone and muscle against bone and muscle, he felt Wetherby's right arm collapse, retreating, absorbing the pressure of Foster's blow by bending before it. And all the while the burly lieutenant kept the death grip with both hands on Foster's neck.

Foster tried the same stroke with his right hand, but with the same result. Wetherby allowed his arm to absorb the impact of the blow by moving his arm backward slightly, but not enough to dislodge his own grip on the black man's neck.

Foster looked into Wetherby's eyes. There was a smile in them. They crinkled at the corners with amusement. Shit, thought Foster, this man's crazy, this crazy honkey is going to strangle me.

Foster's eyes widened in panic. He felt his chest start to ache as the air was slowly being cut off from his lungs. He tried to gasp and suck in air. He could not. He repeated the hand maneuver, both hands punching up, simultaneously this time, but Wetherby pulled him forward by the throat so that Foster's fists struck his own forehead.

The black man brought a knee up hard, trying to strike Wetherby in the groin, anything to make him loosen the grip. But his knee contacted only air. Help, he tried to shout. Let me go, motherfucker, he tried to say but no words came out of his throat. His eyes felt as if they were clouding over. He felt no more urge to attack. He tried again to breathe, but he could not and then he felt a lazy softness pass over his muscles and his eyes closed, as much as he tried to will them to stay open, and then the class saw that he was hanging like a rag doll from the hands of the lieutenant.

Wetherby held on, squeezing, a few seconds longer, then he released his grip and Foster, unconscious, dropped back heavily onto the mat.

The watching rookies murmured.

"Don't worry, he'll be all right," said Wetherby. "But that's a new lesson for you. Don't get fancy, because the minute you do, you're going to meet somebody who's better than you. Do whatever it takes to take your man out and do it quickly and with no regrets. Otherwise, you're going to end up like him." He looked down contemptuously at Foster, who was starting to regain consciousness with some gasping groans. "Or worse," said Wetherby. "If you can imagine that."

He toed Foster. "Okay, Shaft. Up and at 'em."

Still groaning, Foster slowly rolled over from his back onto his stomach, then lifted his knees until he was up in a crawling position. No one moved among the watching recruits until Wetherby nodded. "Give him a hand, somebody," he said.

He looked over the heads of the recruits at two men walking through the door. He felt a tingle in his hands and he sucked a breath deep into the pit of his stomach. Now. At last. It was now.

"All right, men," he said. "That's it for the day. See you tomorrow."

He walked toward the door where he was met by the deputy chief in charge of police training.

"Fred," the man said. "This is Mr. Slote. He's a magazine writer doing a piece on police training procedures."

"Good to meet you," said Wetherby, extending his hand to shake the other man's.

Nothing exceptional, he judged. Thick wrists, but barely six feet tall and slim. He gave away four inches to Wetherby and probably seventy-five pounds, and thick wrists or no, strong for his size or no, it wouldn't be enough, because a strong and good big man beat a strong and good smaller man every time.

Well, almost every time, Wetherby corrected in his mind. There was one little man who was so good that Wetherby would never fool with him. It was strange to think about. Here he was a policeman and dedicated to the law, and somehow he had been pulled outside the law. At first he had told himself he had done it because he wanted the combat secrets the little man had promised him, but now he knew there was another reason, an overwhelming reason. Lieutenant Fred Wetherby did what the little man said because he was afraid not to. It was that simple. And because it was that simple, Wetherby did not have to have any second thoughts about it and he could just stand back and enjoy what he had been told to do. Like kill this puny little Mr. Slote who stood in front of him.

"I'll be glad to show you around," said Wetherby. "We're unusual in police training in that we put so much stress on hand-to-hand combat. Do you know anything about hand-to-hand combat, Mr. Slote?"

"You can call me Remo. No, I don't know anything about it."

"I'll leave you two alone," said the deputy chief. "If you want anything when you leave," he told Remo, "just stop in my office."

"Sure thing, chief. Thanks."

He turned to watch the deputy chief go. Wetherby said, "What happened to your arm?"

Remo put a hand gently up toward his left shoulder. "Talk about clumsy. Would you believe a garage door closed on it?"

"Not really," said Wetherby, meaning the words, but smiling to take away the insult of them.

Remo, annoyed because he had thought he was moving well despite the left arm which he could not move at all today, said, "I've heard a lot about you."

"Oh?"

"Yeah. Fellow in Tenafly. Hawley Bardwell. He said he studied with you."

"Bardwell. Bardwell. I don't know any Bardwell," said Wetherby.

Remo covered his surprise, while deciding that Lieutenant Fred Wetherby was a liar. Lynette Bardwell had name, rank, and serial number. She couldn't have been mistaken about Wetherby.

He said nothing and allowed himself to be shown around the now empty gymnasium. He had started his new life in a gymnasium much like this one. A gym at Folcroft Sanitarium. He had just recovered from an electrocution that wasn't on the level, and someone had put a gun in his hand and promised to let him go if he could shoot an aged Oriental skittering across the gym floor. And because Remo was cocky and young and sure of himself, he accepted the offer and wound up eating splinters from the gym floor.

Wetherby was showing Remo training posts, padded two-by-fours used to teach hand blows, when Remo asked, "Do you find your trainees ever use this knowledge?"

"Sure," said Wetherby. "Think how many times a policeman has to throw a punch to defend himself. How much better is he if he uses something better than a punch?"

"But don't you feel upset about turning men out into the streets who have this terrible weapon in their hands?"

Wetherby smiled at the faggy liberal bleeding heart reporter, and wondered how this Remo Slote had managed to get so much on the bad side of Mr. Winch. He locked the inside gym door as he strolled past the practice posts.

He showed Remo toward the practice mats. "We

train recruits for forty full hours in hand to hand combat."

"Forty hours," said Remo. "Wow, that's a lot."

"Not nearly enough to get good," said Wetherby.

"By the way," said Remo, touching the mat with his right toe, "you didn't tell me where you had trained with Bardwell."

Wetherby stood on the mat facing Remo. They were five feet apart. "I told you, I don't know any Bardwell. Probably just another amateur."

"And you're a professional?" asked Remo.

"Right. Here's why."

One moment, Wetherby was standing, talking. The next moment, he was in the air, heading toward Remo. His right leg was cocked underneath his flying body. Remo recognized the move. The right leg would come into the top part of his body. As Remo fell backward Wetherby would land, and the next step would be a killing hand-blow to Remo's temple.

That was if it was done right.

To be done right, it could not be done to Remo.

Wetherby's leg lashed out. The foot took Remo heavily in the right shoulder.

But there was something wrong with the technique Wetherby had been taught. He could only land the next blow, the killer to the temple, if his opponent went down and didn't strike back.

Remo did not go down. He struck back. He stepped backward one step, saw Wetherby's midsection as open as a church collection basket, and put his own foot into the policeman's solar plexus.

It was over that fast. Wetherby's blow. Pop. Remo's response. Splat.

The look of killing hatred on Wetherby's face changed immediately to a look of puzzled query. His eyes opened wide as if in surprise. He dropped onto his back on the mat. His eyes stayed open.

"Crap," said Remo. "Crap and double crap." Another suicide pilot dead in an attack and Remo still had no information.

And now he had another worry. The fire in his right shoulder, where Wetherby's foot had landed, was spreading through the upper part of his body. He tried to lift his arm. It raised slowly with almost no power. But at least he could still move it. By the next day, he feared he would not even be able to do that. But as long as it worked, he had to use it. He couldn't just waltz out of police headquarters, leaving the dead body of the training officer in the middle of the gym floor.

Slowly, with his right arm held stiffly, he dragged the burly man's body to a supply room at the end of the gym. With every step he took, the pain throbbed more in his shoulder. He felt like screaming now. Another suicide attack. And why?

It was while he was stuffing Lieutenant Wetherby's body into the bottom of a barrel filled with basketballs that he finally understood what it all meant.

He left the gym, disgusted. He had found out nothing, and yet he had found out everything. He was being subject to the traditional Sinanju attack of disrespect.

Two more blows were yet to come.

But he knew no friends of Bardwell, no friends of Wetherby's, and he did not know when or where the third attack might come.

He would have to back go to Lynette Bardwell and try again, look for another name.

But he knew now whose name was already signed to the fourth blow that awaited Remo.

The name was Nuihc. Chiun's nephew, who had vowed death to both Remo and his Korean master.

CHAPTER EIGHT

In Pyongyang, the loss of a people's tank was put before Kim Il Sung, premier of the People's Democratic Republic.

Sung was not from Sinanju, nor was he a believer in the old ways. He was a leader of the new way and he was called comrade by peasant and warrior alike, for he said they were all equal. Still, Sung always wore his warrior uniform with general's boards on his shoulders and a stiff black leather belt.

Sung nodded when he first heard the story. He had heard of the Master of Sinanju, he said. A fairy tale designed to cover the activities of a horde of bandits and cutthroats, he said, and sent a follower named Pak Myoch'ong to go look into the story, for it had been believed that the Masters of Sinanju were of the past, and not a thing for a People's Democratic Republic to worry about.

The first person Pak Myoch'ong took himself to was the governor of the province in which Sinanju was located. The governor had anticipated and dreaded the query because it was he who had instructed the soldiers to confiscate the tribute sent every year by the Master of Sinanju to his own village.

"Why do you question me such?" asked the governor. "Do you doubt that I can rule this province?"

"If the premier doubted you could rule, you would not be governor," Myoch'ong said. "No, I merely ask who are these men who destroy a people's tank with their bare hands."

"It is not I who say so," said the governor. To Myoch'ong it was a denial that any Master of Sinanju existed, so he asked "If not the Master of Sinanju, who?"

"The Americans," said the governor. He pointed out the ship that had been sighted near Sinanju just the week before. And were they not capitalists? And did they not hate the People's Democratic Republic of Korea, and were they not schemers and doers of all manner of evil things?

Myoch'ong said nothing, for he was a wise man and he knew that while it was good for the people that their hatred should be aroused and directed toward someone outside of Pyongyang, nevertheless everytime he heard the word "American" he suspected it was a way of claiming innocence for failing to do one's duty.

So he took himself to Sinanju where there was rejoicing and he said to a child:

"Who is this man called the Master of Sinanju? I would meet with him."

The child took him to a large house at the end of the village's main street. The house was old but made of wood and ivory and stones from other lands, not the weak wood of the Korean countryside.

"How long has this house been here?" he asked the child.

"Forever," said the child, which to Myoch'ong meant only a long time because he knew children. But such was the look of the house, the mix of styles from many lands and cultures, that he said to himself, yes, this house is very old. It is the history of many races; it is the history of man.

Even though Myoch'ong was a server of the new way from his youngest days, when he entered the house he bowed and took off his shoes in the old way, which his people had taken from the Japanese. He bowed to an old man with white beard whose hands had fingernails grown long in the manner of the ancients, and the old man said:

"Who are you that I have not seen you in the village?"

Myoch'ong answered that he was from Pyongyang and served Kim Il Sung, and asked if the old man were truly the Master of Sinanju "of whom many wonders are spoken."

"I am the one of whom you speak," said Chiun.

"I have heard that with but your hands you are more powerful than the people's tank."

"That is true."

"How can it be true? Steel is harder than flesh."

"The greatest weapon is the human mind. A tank is but a tool and no better than the mind that uses it."

"But fools can destroy wise men with it."

"I say unto you, young man, that there are wise men and there are wiser men. But the wisest among them has learned only that he has not uncovered the true strength of his mind. Even a fool who uses his mind is stronger than a wise man who does not."

Myoch'ong admitted his confusion and Chiun said:

"You seek a man of miracles. Yet the greatest miracle is man himself. And this I know and this you do not know and this your Pyongyangers in the people's tank did not know and now they sit in the sand like empty shells."

"I still do not understand," said Myoch'ong. "But perhaps our premier will. I would take you to him."

Chiun waved his hand in dismissal. "Sinanju does not come to Pyongyang. Return to your loose women and wine."

But Myoch'ong was not ready to leave.

"If you have such great wisdom, why do you not seek to share it with your people? Why do you sit here in this house alone, with none but this serving girl?"

"Can an ocean fill a teacup? Can the sky fill a bowl? So it is that Sinanju cannot be given everyone."

"But it is given many."

"Few," said Chiun.

"I am told that you are not the only Master of Sinanju."

"There is a pretender named Nuihc who calls himself Uinch or Winch or Chuni. All these are the same. He is one man, the son of my brother."

"See. So you share with him."

"That share will soon be removed," said Chiun, "and removed so thoroughly its remover will be white. This I say to you. The heart is the first home of the House of Sinanju, and when I found none of ours worthy, I gave it to a white man."

"An American?" said Myoch'ong, disclosing his worst fears.

"One I found eating hamburgers and drinking alcohol and other poisons. Weak in mind and body, but his heart was good. To him I have given all. From a pale piece of pig's ear, I have made him Sinanju."

103

Myoch'ong glanced about the room and saw a photograph of a pale-faced man, framed in gold, with western handwriting across the photo, and he asked Chiun if this were the white man of whom he spoke.

"No," said Chiun. "That is an artist of great skill. That is Rad Rex who in the daytime dramas of the Americans performs with genius and brilliance in a great drama called *As the Planet Revolves*. That is his signature on the picture. In America, I have many important friends."

Myoch'ong thought quickly, then again asked if Chiun would not come to Pyongyang to see Premier Kim Il Sung himself and receive an autographed picture of the premier which the whole village could appreciate and put in a place of honor.

But Chiun answered: "When has Kim Il Sung ever worried about Mary Lambert's operation at the hands of the illegitimate son of Blake Winfield's stepdaughter, the one who discovered that Carson Magnum, the mayor, was addicted to heroin and had taken payoffs from Winfield himself never to expose the abortion ring which had almost killed Mary when she was pregnant with the child of the unknown father?"

"It was not his fault," said Myoch'ong. "If Kim Il Sung had known of these things, he would have worried too."

"It is a ruler's duty to know many things," said Chiun, dismissing Myoch'ong with a wave of his hand and setting his face toward the window, beyond which was the sea.

Myoch'ong puzzled over those things that night and finally summoned seven soldiers of great strength to his side. "Whoever slays the Master of Sinanju will be made colonel if he is major and general if he is colonel," he said.

The soldiers nodded and grinned, and armed with guns and knives set off for Chiun's house, because each wanted to be the one to win promotion.

In the morning, none had returned to Myoch'ong, so he went himself to Chiun's house to see what the seven had done. Entering the house, he saw not a tapestry or trinket disturbed. Chiun sat upon his cushion, unharmed, and told Myoch'ong: "That which you have sent has returned to the earth. Go now and tell your master in the whore city Pyongyang that the Master of Sinanju will see him if he will bring tribute."

What kind of tribute, Myoch'ong asked.

"First, take all Pyongyangers from this province. Second, chastise the evil governor who has usurped the tribute due this village. Third, a message should be sent to America that the great dramas will be happily received. There are ways to do this and Americans know them. Your premier should invite such men as can do this to Korea. He should treat them well, for if they are treated well perhaps even Rad Rex himself may come. These things are possible."

And Myoch'ong left with heavy heart for he knew Kim Il Sung would not invite Americans into his land again. When he appeared before the premier, he told him of what he had seen and of the seven men who were no more. The premier was angered and purposed the sending of an army against Sinanju, but Myoch'ong bade him delay for he had heard tales

105

of how neither wall nor steel nor human arm could stop the Masters of Sinanju, and that through the ages their special talent had been the elimination of heads of state. Or, he added shrewdly, of those who would be heads of state.

And King Il Sung paused and thought, and then he asked where Myoch'ong heard these things. And to this, Myoch'ong answered he had read of them in old manuscripts that told of Sinanju.

"Reactionary feudal fairy tales designed to suppress the aspirations of the masses. Sinanju has always been a home for bandits and murderers and thieves," said Kim Il Sung.

But Myoch'ong reminded him of the seven soldiers and of the people's tank and disclosed to him the corruption of the governor of the province.

Yet this did not dissuade the premier. But when Myoch'ong said that the Master of Sinanju had taught his secrets to a white, an American, and might teach more Americans these things, the premier dismissed everyone from his conference room but Myoch'ong.

And quietly, so that even the walls could not hear, he said to Myoch'ong: "I would see this bandit. I shall go with you to him. But this I warn you. Should he be but another lackey of the imperialists, you will be denounced before the presidium and the politboro."

"This one is not a lackey of anyone."

"Good. On the way you will tell me what he wants of us, should there be such demands."

Now Myoch'ong was not a fool, and every time the premier asked what the Master of Sinanju desired, Myoch'ong saw a pleasant field to look at, or wondered about the strength of the people's army, or brought up the Japanese whom everyone hated.

And again Myoch'ong returned to the house of the Master of Sinanju and asked permission to enter. And Kim Il Sung, seeing Myoch'ong bowing in the old manner, spat upon the floor.

"A den of feudalism," he said.

"Pigs and horses dribble on floors. That is why they are kept in barns," said the Master of Sinanju.

"Do you know who I am, old man? I am Kim Il Sung."

"And I am Chiun."

"Watch your mouth, Chiun."

"It is not I who drivels on floors. You get your manners from Russians."

"You are a bandit and a lackey of imperialists," said the premier without caution, for he was angered greatly.

"Were you not the premier of our people in the north," said Chiun, "I would slay you like a pig for dinner. Yet I withhold my hand for I would reason with you."

"How can a lackey reason?" said the premier. "All his reason serves his white masters. I serve Korea."

"Before you, young man," said Chiun, "Sinanju was. During the Mongol invasion, Sinanju was. During the Chinese lords, Sinanju was. During the Japanese lords, Sinanju was. During the Russian lords, Sinanju was. They are all gone and we are here as we will be here after Kim Il Sung was. But I would speak with you for, lo, after these many years Korea has a leader who is of her own. And that is you, although you are but a Pyongyanger."

And hearing these words, Sung sat. But he neither bowed nor did he remove his shoes as in the old ways. And Myoch'ong listened with great apprehension. But when Chiun spoke, he knew all would be well for there was much wisdom in the Master.

"You come here seeking the wisdom of Sinanju, otherwise why would a premier come to this poor village?" said Chiun.

And Sung agreed.

"You call me lackey," said Chiun.

And Sung agreed.

"Yet who is the lackey? Have I joined Sinanju to the Russians? Have I made compacts with the Chinese? Do I on every occasion support Arab and African and even whites just because they profess a belief in one form of government?"

"They are our allies," said Sung. "The Russians give us arms. The Chinese fought Americans for us."

And Chiun smiled.

"The Russians gave arms because they hate the Americans. The Chinese fought because they hate the Americans. Lucky are we that these two hate each other for they would sit in Pyongyang and not you. As for Africans, Arabs, and whites, they are far away and not even yellow. The Japanese are greedy, the Chinese despicable, the Russians swine, and as for our own southerners, they would sleep with ducks if birds had big enough openings."

At this, Sung roared in laughter.

"This man has a proper outlook," he said to Myoch'ong. "Who is responsible for calling him a lackey? Who has given me such misinformation?"

And Chiun spoke again. "But we must look with more sympathy upon our southern brothers because they are of the south and cannot help themselves. This is their nature."

Myoch'ong gasped. For never had anyone dared

say any kind thing about those beneath the thirty-eighth parallel.

"I too have often thought such. They cannot help being what they are," said Sung.

"And Pyongyang is not the nicest of places. It is where good people go wrong," said Chiun.

"I was not born in Pyongyang but in Hamhung," said Sung.

"A fine village," said Chiun.

"Sinanju is fine also," said Sung.

"I am of Paekom," said Myoch'ong.

"But he has risen above it," said Sung.

"Some of our best friends come from Paekom. They transcend their origins," said Chiun.

Now Kim Il Sung was satisfied that here was a man of good heart and proper thinking. But he was troubled.

"I hear you teach Sinanju to whites. To an American."

Now Chiun knew this to be a great offense, one that could not be laid before the premier with all honesty, so he was careful with his words, and he spoke with slowness and with caution.

"In my own village, in my own family, none I found was worthy. There was laxness and sloth and deceit. Among ourselves, we can admit these things."

Sung nodded for he too knew of the problems of governing.

"There was ingratitude for what was offered," said Chiun.

How well did Sung know this also.

"There was backsliding and lack of discipline," said Chiun.

Oh, how truly did the Master of Sinanju know this, proclaimed Sung.

"The son of my own brother took the preciousness given him and used it for selfish gain."

How well did Sung know this trait. He looked somberly at Myoch'ong.

"He acted like a southerner, "said Chiun.

Sung spat and this time Chiun nodded approval. For it was a proper moment for such things.

"And so I sought another, that this knowledge of our people should not die."

"A wise thing," said Sung.

"I would have chosen one of us. But in all the village, in all the North, I did not find one with a Korean heart. I did not know you at the time."

"I had my problems," said Sung.

"So I sought a Korean heart like yours. One of us."

"Good for you," said Sung, placing a strong hand on the shoulder of the Master of Sinanju by way of congratulation.

"This man of our heart happened to have suffered a misfortune at birth. A catastrophe."

Sung's countenance became exceeding sad.

"What was this misfortune?"

"He was born white and American."

Sung gasped at the horror.

"Each morning he had to look at his round eyes in the mirror. Each meal he had to eat hamburger. Each day, naught but others with that same affliction for company."

"And what did you?"

"I found him and saved him from the Americans. From their thinking and ill manners."

"You did well," said Sung. But Myoch'ong, being of a suspicious nature, asked how Chiun knew this was not just another American but a Korean heart in an American body.

110

"Because he learned correctness exceeding well, and to prove the point he will demonstrate what he has learned when he comes to honor his heritage here in Sinanju."

"How do we know," asked Myoch'ong, "that it is not just an American to whom you have taught all of Sinanju?"

"An American?" said Chiun with a scoffing laugh. "Did you not see Americans in the great war with the south? Did you not see Americans when you had them with their ship? An American?"

"Some Americans are hard," said Myoch'ong. But so taken with the words of the Master was Kim Il Sung that he forgot his own truth and looked at Myoch'ong with scorn. Of course, this white man has a Korean heart, he said.

"His name is Remo," said Chiun.

And thus it was that evening, in the large People's Building in Pyongyang, when the name Remo was mentioned again to the Premier, Kim Il Sung recognized it. He was told a message had been received that an American named Remo would be disgraced in the village of Sinanju, and that he would be disgraced by a man named Nuihc.

And the sender of this message was himself Nuihc and he pledged the devotion of his soul to Kim Il Sung and the People's Democratic Republic of Korea. And he signed his message in this fashion:

"Nuihc, Master of Sinanju."

CHAPTER NINE

"I'd like a million dollars, lady, in singles. "Don't count it, weigh it."

Lynette Bardwell looked up at her teller's cage and smiled at Remo.

"Hiya," she said. "Missed you last night."

"You were among the missing last night," Remo said. "But I thought there's always tonight. You almost done here?"

Lynette looked at the clock in the center of the bank lobby, high up over Remo's head. The craning of her neck caused her bosom to rise.

"Ten minutes more."

"Dinner okay? Your husband won't mind."

"I guess he won't," said Lynette. "I haven't heard from him. I guess he did go away for awhile."

Remo waited in front and Lynette came boobily bobbing out in precisely ten minutes.

"Take my car?" she said. Remo added. In her car in the parking lot, she leaned over to brush his cheek with her lips. The top of her body pressed against his right shoulder. Remo grimaced.

"What's the matter? You hurt your shoulder?"

Remo nodded.

"How'd that happen?"

"Would you believe I ran into a barrel of basketballs?"

"No."

"Good. Don't."

Lynette drove and Remo picked the dinner spot this time, an even darker restaurant than the night before, but one that looked as if it could cook rice.

It could, and Remo joined Lynette in eating.

"Did you see Wetherby?" she asked.

"Yes. But he couldn't help."

"Couldn't help you what? You know I don't know what it is you're after."

"I'm doing a book on Oriental fighting. Your husband, Wetherby, they all have some special training, something unique. I know enough about it to know that. But they won't tell. I think I've stumbled onto some new training secret, and, well, I'm stubborn."

"I wish I could help," she said, picking over a piece of crabmeat. "But it's not my bag."

"What is your bag?"

The crabmeat vanished into her mouth without a trace. "I'm a lover, not a fighter."

Over her brandy, Lynette confided that her husband had never stayed away at night before. "You didn't scare him away, did you?"

"Do I look like I could scare anybody away?"

Remo picked slowly at his rice, first using his right hand, then his left. The pain in his shoulders was growing, and each time he brought the fork to his mouth he could feel the burning heat of injury moving through the shoulder joint, throbbing its pain into his consciousness. If only Chiun were in the States, instead of gallivanting around in Sinanju, he might be able to help. Someplace in that memory of his would be a way to make Remo's arms work again, someplace a way to stop the pain and the weakness.

113

And these were just the first two blows. He knew now that he had been targeted by Nuihc, the nephew of Chiun, who sought Chiun's title and had vowed Remo's death. Already Remo's arms were gone, worthless. What was next?

Finally eating wasn't worth the pain, and Remo just let the fork drop from his fingers. He found himself nodding at Lynette without hearing what she was saying, and soon they were driving toward her house and he heard himself accept her offer to stay in her upstairs spare room so he could rest.

And he felt so badly he no longer tried to maintain any pretense by asking if her husband might object. The husband was dead, and fuck 'im, he had hurt Remo's arm and he couldn't rot in that coffin fast enough to suit Remo.

Lynette helped him upstairs to a big bedroom in her house and he let her undress him. She did it slowly, trailing her fingers over his body and she put him naked under the covers. She was soft but efficient and Remo thought it rather marvelous how she had learned to hold her liquor much better than she had the night before. That was funny. Funny, funny, Remo thought. Look, look, look at funny Remo.

He could not move his upper body. The pain surged through his shoulders and down his arms, numbing his fingertips, into his chest where it seemed to attack each one of his ribs. into his neck where it made movement painful.

Hurt, hurt Remo. Look, look, look at hurt, hurt Remo.

He was hallucinating. It had been so long since he had suffered pain, real pain. For most people, pain

114

was a helpful warning sign that something was wrong with the body and the owner should take care of it. But Remo was one with his body, it was not a belonging but a being, and he did not have to be reminded when there was something wrong with his body, and so there was no need for him to pain. He had almost forgotten what pain felt like. He had felt pain when he sat in the electric chair. They had failed to fry him, but at least they had given him a quick braising. That was pain. And so was this. In between those two times, in all the ten years, there hadn't been too much other pain to remember.

Look, look, look, funny Remo. He was losing control.

Look, look, Remo, look at the beautiful lady walking through the door. Look at the white nylon gown she's wearing that you can see through.

Look at the soft swelling of the highrise breasts, look at the smooth round outlines of her body, silhouetted against the hall light. Look at the long tan legs. Look how she smiles at you, Remo. The lovely lady likes you, Remo. She will make you feel all better. Remo wanted to feel all better. He smiled.

Lynette leaned over him in the bed. "I will make you feel better," she said.

Remo kept smiling, because it hurt to stop. "Make me feel better. Want to feel better. Arms hurt."

"Where do they hurt, Remo?" Lynette asked. "Here?" She touched his left shoulder through the strand of muscles in the front and Remo groaned with the pain.

"Or here?"

She touched his right shoulder with her fingertips and pressed and Remo screamed.

"Hurt. Hurt," he shouted.

"There, there. Lynette will make you feel better," she said.

Remo opened his eyes narrowly. The tall blonde woman he had made a widow was standing next to the bed, and then with a smooth practiced swoop she was lifting her negligee over her head.

She held it in her fingertips at arm's length, her eyes seemingly fastened to his by wires, and then she dropped the negligee into a soft fluttery mound on the floor.

She moved closer to Remo, ran fingers down his cheeks, trailed them down his neck, and then pulled the blanket down from his unclad body.

No, he wanted to say. No. No sex. Don't feel well. No sex.

But Lynette Bardwell was moving her fingers all over his body now, and he found that if he concentrated on something other than his shoulders, the pain was not so severe, so he concentrated on that part of the body that Lynette was concentrating on and then Remo was ready. Lynette smiled and moved up onto the bed and was over him and then on him and then surrounding him, swallowing him with her body.

She knelt over Remo looking down at him and her face was smiling but there was no mirth in the showing of her teeth, which looked as if they were about to bite, and there was a glitter in her eyes, a kind of merciless sparkle, and she began to move her body and it helped, it helped, it helped if he moved his a little, and he stopped thinking of his shoulders

116

and thought only of himself and Lynette and their junction.

He wanted to move his hands up to her, to reach her body, but he could not. His hands and arms were straight at his side, pinned there by her thighs straddling him, but he still had some movement in his fingers and he used them to touch the insides of her thighs where there were large clusters of nerves, very delicately throbbing.

His fingers brought her to life. Her eyes opened wider and she began moving on him faster, wilder, and it was better, better than the pain in his arms, and he wasn't thinking of the pain anymore. The pain had come from two people who had tried to disable him before killing him, and the next blow would be someone coming after one of his legs, but he couldn't, he wouldn't think about that now.

Lynette was sitting up straight, and she threw her head back and laughed, a loud rolling laugh, and then she looked down at him, and for the first time Remo focused on her eyes and saw the meaning in them, and she let her body fall forward, her head toward his face, but she caught herself with her two hands, slamming them against his shoulders, like an athlete doing pushups.

The pain shot through his body and Remo screamed. And she twisted her arm muscles and the hard heels of her hands ground into his shoulder joints. She laughed again and leaned her face close to his.

He felt his face was wet. She was crying? No, he was crying, crying in pain.

"You killed my husband," she said. It was not a question.

"And you killed Wetherby," she said. She twisted her hands again into his shoulders.

Hurt. Hurt. Have to get away.

"But they damaged you. And I'm going to damage you worse. And the little bit that's going to be left of you will go to Nuihc. In a bag."

Nuihc? She knew. Lynette was the third kamikaze. The third shot was hers. Did she know that Nuihc planned for her to die? That Remo was supposed to kill her? But he couldn't kill her. He couldn't move.

"You know Nuihc?" Remo gasped.

"I serve Nuihc," she corrected. "Hawley was a fool. Wetherby was a brute. But Nuihc is a man. He loves me. He said the best blow in Scotland was mine. I was the best."

She continued moving the lower half of her body up and down, using Remo as an instrument for her pleasure and his pain, and all he could do was keep his fingers going inside her thighs.

"Mr. Winch is a man," she said.

He felt her voice soften and her muscles begin to tense, then relax, in an unconscious rhythm she could not control.

"The kind of man you might have been. Ohhh. Ohhhh."

She was bucking on Remo now like a bareback cowboy on a crazed horse. He was pinned and powerless and in pain from her hands on his shoulders. She screamed a heavy gasping scream of pleasure and said "Oh, Nuihc, Nuihc," and when she stopped, she said, "You could have been a man, too. If you had lived."

And then her creamed wet body moved up off Remo and he could feel the blessed relief of her small fists withdrawing from the points of pain on his shoulders and he could open his eyes again. He saw her standing on the bed, looking down at his body below her bare legs, and he saw her curl her left leg up under her, standing as if she were a flamingo, and then she drew the other leg up, too, and her body crashed down, aimed at the long rope of muscle in the front of his right thigh, and even before she landed, Remo could sense what the excruciating pain would be like, and then her body hit, and it seemed to land in slow motion. First there was the touch of contact, then pressure, then pain as her weight and skill tore open the long lifting muscle of the thigh.

"First you," she yelled, "and after you, the old man."

Purely by reflex, purely by training, purely by instinct, knowing it meant nothing because he was going to die, Remo rolled his left leg toward the far wall, so the knee was pointing outward, then with all the effort and strength he had left, he rolled the knee back inward toward his own right leg, toward Lynette Bardwell, who knelt on his right leg, her face exultant with the glow of victory, and he drove the knee across his own body and heard the crack as it found her temple bone.

Lynette still smiled. She looked at Remo, smiling, and then, for just a brief second, the smile turned into a look of pain, and in that moment Remo knew that she suddenly suspected that Nuihc, whom she thought loved her, had guessed that she would die here, and then she could no longer worry about things like that because her thin temple bones were driven into her brain by the force of Remo's driving knee, and the smile and the look of pain both withered, like a time-lapse photo study of a flower's life and death, and Lynette fell forward onto Remo's chest and died.

He felt the warm sticky ooze from her head drip onto his chest. It felt warm. Warm. And warm was good and he wanted to be warm, so he didn't have chills. And the pain in both shoulders and the pain in his right thigh all hurt, and he closed his eyes and decided it would be nice to sleep.

And if he died that would be nice, too, because then he would always be warm. And he wouldn't hurt anymore.

CHAPTER TEN

Remo woke.

He had slept to forget something, and now he remembered it. The pain in his shoulders and arms.

And there was something wrong with his legs.

A weight was on them. He looked down toward his legs, but he couldn't see them. Right under his chin, grinning up at him, was the wide-eyed, open-mouthed, bloodied head of Lynette Bardwell.

Remo remembered.

"Hi, toots," he said. "Read any good karate books lately?"

Carefully, Remo slid his left leg out from under the woman, then with his left leg he pushed her. Her body rolled down from his right leg onto the bed, then slipped onto the floor where it hit with a brittle, cold thump.

Remo swung his body around, extended his legs to the floor, stood up, and collapsed onto the gray tweed rug as his right leg buckled under him.

And just that much effort brought back the pain, like a toothache that seems to have been cured by a night's sleep, but starts throbbing before you get out of bed.

Remo crawled toward the wall and then using the wall as a brace managed to get himself into an upright position. Trying to put no weight on his right leg, using it just for steering, he hobbled to the bathroom and, hammering with his powerless arms, was able to get the shower turned on.

He hoisted himself into the shower and stood there a long time, unable to soap himself, but letting the water wash Lynette Bardwell's dried blood off his body.

The warm water washed away some of his pain, too, and Remo was able to think. Nuihc was coming after him. The next attack, the fourth blow, would be deadly.

He got out of the shower, leaving the water running. He stopped in front of the bathroom mirror and looked at his own image. "You're kinda young to die," he told the face that looked back at him. But the face didn't seem frightened; it seemed puzzled as if it were trying to remember something. Looking at the face was like looking at a stranger, and that stranger was puzzled. There was something in the back of his mind, some tiny memory that he knew he should remember. But what was it?

Remo dragged on his pants and congratulated himself on wearing a button-front shirt because at least he could slip his arms into it. Yesterday's pullover would have been out of the question.

What was it?

Something Lynette had said. Something.

What?

What?

"After you . . ." After Remo, what? What?

"After you," she had said. "After you," and then he remembered as the words jumped back into his ears as if someone were shouting at him.

She had said:

"After you, the old man."

Chiun.

Remo hobbled to the telephone. He was able to cradle the phone between left ear and shoulder and, thanking God for pushbutton dials, banged out an 800-area code toll-free number.

"Yes?" came the lemony voice.

"Remo. What time is it?"

"It's two-twelve P.M., and this is an unauthorized time for you to call. Don't you remember that. . . ."

"I need help. I'm hurt."

In Folcroft Sanitarium, Dr. Harold W. Smith sat up straight in his chair. In ten years he had never heard those words from Remo.

"Hurt? How?"

"Muscles torn. I can't drive. Send someone for me."

"Where are you?"

"Home of Lynette Bardwell. Tenafly, New Jersey. You can tell me from Lynette 'cause I'm still alive."

"Are you in any danger of compromise?" asked Smith.

"That's it, Smitty. Good for you. Up the organization. Worry about security."

"Yes," said Smith noncommittally. "Is there any danger?"

"I don't know." Remo sighed. It hurt to talk and now the telephone was hurting his shoulder where it rested. "If the security of this operation depends on me, start looking for a new job."

"Stay where you are, Remo. Help is coming."

Smith listened. There was no joking, no wisecracking in Remo's voice this time, as he said: "Hurry."

123

Smith rose, carefully buttoned his jacket, and walked from his office. He told his secretary he would be gone for the rest of the day, which announcement she greeted with open-mouthed astonishment. Dr. Smith, in the past ten years, took off only every other Friday afternoon, and on those days he arrived early in the office and worked through his lunch hour, so he had already put in his full eight hours before leaving for his golf date at the nearby country club. A date which, she had one day learned, he kept with himself, playing alone.

He boarded a medical helicopter on the sanitarium grounds and was flown to Teterboro Airport in New Jersey where he rented a Ford Mustang, even though a Volkswagen was cheaper and there would be one available in just an hour or so and he liked the Volkswagen's gas economy.

With the help of a telephone directory and the driver of a mail truck, he found the Bardwell house. He parked behind a brown Ford in the driveway and went to the side door leading to the kitchen. No one answered his knocking. The door was unlocked.

Smith entered a kitchen filled with plastic clocks that looked like fried eggs sunnyside up, cooked too long, and with ceramic spoon rests that looked like smiling babies, and with coffee, sugar, and flour canisters that looked like overgrown soup cans, and a room in which everything looked like something else.

Smith had no mind for philosophy so it did not occur to him that a vast portion of America made its living by making things look like other things, and that this was a little strange because it might have been better to make the first things good-looking enough so that they had no need for disguises.

The lean pinched-face man moved quietly through the first floor of the house, efficiently searching the rooms, the kitchen, dining room, the living room, the bath, the television room in the back, decorated with a shelf holding a collection of plaques and trophies from karate competitions, set up in rows, that looked like nothing so much as an advancing army of Oriental men and women fighting their way through unfriendly air to reach their enemies.

He found Remo upstairs on the floor of the bedroom, lying next to the bed. Next to him was the body of a naked blonde woman, her face and head caked with dried brown blood.

Smith knelt quickly next to Remo and put his hand inside Remo's open shirt. He saw Remo's mouth move into a grimace of pain. Smith looked at his watch. He counted the heartbeats for fifteen seconds. Twelve. He multiplied by four. Remo's pulse was forty-eight.

If that had been Smith's pulse rate, he would have rushed to a cardiologist. But Smith, who read his medical bulletins on CURE personnel like a financier read the stock market tables, knew that for Remo a pulse of forty-eight was in the normal range.

"Remo," he said.

Remo's eyes opened slowly.

"Can you walk?" Smith asked. "We've got to get out of here."

"Hi, Smitty. Keep an eye on the paper clips. Every time you turn your back, someone's stealing them."

"Remo, you've got to get up."

"Get up. Right. Got to get up. Can't go lying down on government time."

He closed his eyes again.

Smith put his left arm under Remo's thighs and his right arm across the top of Remo's right arm and under his back and hoisted Remo into his arms. He was surprised, despite himself, at how light Remo was. He had weighed two hundred pounds when the organization had found him ten years ago, and Smith had known that his weight had come down some forty pounds, but like all gradual weight losses it had not been visible.

Leaning backward to counteract Remo's weight in his arms, Dr. Smith descended the steps to the first floor. Every time he reached his foot down to touch a new step, the slight jar to his body brought a squint of pain into the corner's of Remo's closed eyes.

In the kitchen, Smith deposited Remo into a chair at the kitchen table, then went outside to start the car's motor and drive it up as close as he could to the kitchen door.

He opened the passenger's door. When he got back into the kitchen, Remo's eyes were open.

"Hi, Smitty. Took you long enough to get here."

"Yes."

"I must have called you hours ago and here you are, taking your time about things, while I'm feeling rotten."

"Yes," said Smith.

"How'd I get to the kitchen?" asked Remo.

"You probably walked," said Smith. "Just as you're going to walk to that car outside."

"I can't walk, Smitty."

126

"Hobble then. You don't think I'm going to carry you, do you?"

"Not you, Smitty. That's laborers' work. Do you WASPS go to a school where you learn to be obnoxious?"

"When you finish feeling sorry for yourself, I'll be out in the car," Smith said coldly. "I suggest you hurry up."

Smith waited in the car, an unusual feeling of disquiet within him. He wished that he could have told Remo he was concerned about him, but he did not know how. Years of training, years of service, years of administration in that strange government underworld where a man who was your friend for years one day just stopped coming around, vanished, swallowed up, gone, and no one ever spoke of him again, as if he had never existed in the first place.

It was just too long-standing a tradition for Smith to be able to violate.

He watched as Remo came out onto the small kitchen porch. He tried first to hold onto the stair railing with his right hand, but he winced and gave that up. He put his right hip against the railing, then hopped down a step, landing on his left foot. Then he leaned sideways, right hip against the railing, until he was balanced and ready for his next lunge down.

Remo made it, hopping, to the car, and slid in through the open door. Smith reached across him, pulled the door shut, and backed carefully out of the driveway. He drove as quickly as the speed laws of New Jersey permitted, out of the town, onto Route 4, heading for the George Washington Bridge.

Only when he was on the highway did he ask Remo what had happened.

"There was a girl in the upstairs bedroom . . ."

"I saw her."

"Right. She disabled my right leg."

"And your arms?"

"Shoulders, Smitty. Two other guys did that."

"But how?" asked Smith. "I thought you were trained to stop that sort of thing from happening."

"Suicide attacks," said Remo. "Anyway, I need something."

"Yes. A doctor," said Smith.

"I need a submarine."

"What?"

"A sub. I'm going to Sinanju."

"Why? Remember, you're supposed to be checking out the death of one of our programmers."

"Remember the blows he suffered that mashed his joints?"

"Yes."

"I've had three of them so far. The fourth is due in Sinanju."

"I don't understand," said Smith.

And because Remo did not understand either, did not know how he knew what he knew, he said, "You don't have to. But Chiun is in danger and I've got to go to Sinanju."

"What good are you going to be to him? You can't even walk."

"I'll think of something. I'd rather be near him."

Smith drove on mechanically, not distinctively enough to be called good driver or bad driver.

A few minutes later, he said:

"Sorry, Remo, you can't go. I can't allow it."

"I'll pay for the gas myself, Smitty."

"Chiun is different," Smith explained. "He's a Korean. But you're an American. If you're captured in North Korea by the government there, it can cause an international incident. Not to mention blowing our whole apparatus. We'll have to close down."

"And what do you think you'll have to do if the *New York Times* gets a letter tomorrow listing locations, places, dates, killings, government interference? There was that business in Miami, remember? And the labor union. What will happen to you then?" asked Remo.

Smith drove on glumly.

"That's blackmail," he said.

"Company policy."

"Extortion," said Smith.

"Company policy."

"A naked unprincipled threat," said Smith.

"That's the biz, sweetheart," said Remo.

Smith pulled off the highway at a motel outside White Plains and, with a key from a ring in his pocket, opened the door of a room the organization rented year-round. He helped Remo into the room, located in the back of the building, secure from the street, helped Remo onto the bed, then left. He was back in twenty-five minutes with a man in a business suit, carrying a leather medical bag.

The doctor examined Remo carefully.

Remo would not cooperate. "I don't need all this," he told Smith in a hiss. "Chiun can fix me up."

The doctor called Smith into a corner of the room for consultation.

"This man belongs in a hospital," he said softly. "Both shoulders are separated. The major muscles in the right thigh are actually ripped. The pain must be excruciating. Frankly, Doctor, I think you overstepped yourself by removing him from the scene of the accident. He should have been carried by ambulance from the wreck."

Smith nodded as if he agreed with the lecture. "Patch him up as best you can until I convince him to get to the hospital, please."

The doctor nodded.

Despite Remo's total lack of enthusiasm, he bandaged Remo's shoulders, restricting his arm movements even further, but guaranteeing that the separated muscles would have time to knit before being abused. He also bandaged Remo's right thigh heavily. His last act was to reach into his bag and withdraw a hypodermic syringe.

"I'm going to give you something for the pain," he said.

Remo shook his head. "No, you're not."

"But the pain must be terrible. This will just help to relieve it."

"No needles," said Remo. "Smitty, remember that hamburger that put me in the hospital? No needles. No drugs in the system."

Smith looked at the doctor and shook his head. "He'll deal with the pain, doctor. No injections."

Smith escorted the doctor to the door and outside on the walkway thanked him for his assistance.

"Don't mention it," said the doctor, who had not come willingly, but only because his hospital director had told him if he did not go on this case he might find someday that he had trouble in obtaining his specialty licenses. The medical director of the hospital had said this because he had been advised that it would be beneficial in the ongoing review of his income tax returns to make sure that a doctor was available for a motel call, in exactly three minutes.

When Smith reentered the room, Remo was sitting up on the bed.

"Okay, Smitty, where is it?"

"Where is what?"

"My submarine."

"One thing at a time."

"Anybody who can get a doctor to make a house call won't have any trouble getting a submarine to sneak me into North Korea."

And with that, Remo closed his eyes and lay back to rest.

He would soon be on his way to Sinanju; he had done all he could; the next thing was to warn Chiun about the danger from Nuihc. It was only as he drifted into sleep that he allowed himself to remember that it was Remo himself who had drawn the first three blows from Nuihc's kamikazes, and the next blow, under the ages-old tradition of Sinanju, would mean Remo's death.

And after Remo, Chiun.

CHAPTER ELEVEN

Captain Lee Enright Leahy of the U.S. Submarine *Darter* thought it was all very funny. Sneaking into enemy waters, putting ashore a man old enough to be Confucius, sneaking away, and what kind of a man was the old Oriental? A man who wanted to watch soap operas and was annoyed that Navy submarines did not have TV reception facilities for *As the Planet Revolves*.

Captain Leahy thought this all very funny, so funny in fact that he was in the process of telling it to his fellow drinkers at the officers' club bar at Mindanao, where the Navy maintained a small base to refuel submarines.

But he had not gotten quite to the good part, the part about the soap operas, when he was tapped on the shoulder by a chief petty officer.

"Cap'n, sir."

"What is it?" Leahy said, his voice surly at being interrupted.

"Phone call, sir."

"Tell them I'll be there in a minute."

"It's Washington, sir."

The CPO's voice was insistent.

The moment was gone; the officers who had been listening with rapt attention were now turning back toward each other, picking up the threads of their own conversations. Damn, thought Leahy. Aloud he said, "probably another ferry run for another old gook who likes soap operas," but the comment did not get the rise he had hoped for and Captain Leahy went to the phone.

There he was told by an official in the Navy Department that he would be presented with a passenger who would have sealed orders. Leahy would follow the orders. He would not mention this to anyone as the orders were top secret and so was the mission.

And he was directed to return to his ship immediately to await the arrival of the passenger.

Annoyed, without even time to finish his drink, Captain Leahy, jaw set, marched out of the officers' club and walked the hundred yards to the pier where the *Darter* had been refueled and made ready for another voyage. The long oil and supply hoses that were used to revitalize the sub's innards had been dropped from the feeder holes as the sub lay tied up at dockside. Refueling, resupply was over.

Captain Leahy clambered up the gangway to the deck of the sub where he was met by his executive officer.

"We've taken aboard a passenger," the exec said.

Leahy shook his head. "Another Charley Chan?" he asked.

"No, sir, this one's an American. Young. Or I think he's young. He seems to be injured. He walks with a cane. I've put him in my quarters, sir."

"All right, Lieutenant. I'd better go see what nitty-witty the U.S. Government is up to tonight."

Captain Leahy went down the forward hatch and knocked on the door of the passenger's compartment.

133

"Yeah?"

"The captain."

"What do you want?"

"I'm coming in to talk to you."

"If you want to."

When Leahy opened the door, the new passenger was lying on the built-in bunk, wearing jockey shorts. Both shoulders were heavily bandaged, his right thigh was wrapped around with bandages. A cane leaned against the small built-in writing desk. The passenger's clothes were strewn on the floor.

"Don't tell me," Leahy said. "We're taking you to the Rusk Institute for Physical Rehabilitation." He smiled at his own joke. He was the only one who did.

"No, actually you're taking me to Sinanju." The passenger nodded his head toward the desk. "It's all in those orders over there."

Leahy opened the sealed envelope marked "top secret." The orders were identical to those he had received for the old Oriental.

"Is your luggage aboard?" asked Leahy.

"I don't travel with luggage."

"That's a novelty."

"And I don't like soap operas," said Remo.

"That's a novelty, too."

"And another novelty is that I don't like company, I don't feel like chit-chat, I won't complain about the food because all I want is rice unseasoned, and I won't complain about the air or the noise or the boredom as long as we get out of here and get to Sinanju as quickly as possible."

"My sentiments exactly."

134

"See you there," said Remo. "I'm going to sleep."

And that was the last Captain Leahy saw or heard of his passenger until they were in the West Korean Bay and he had to go to the passenger's cabin to tell him they were soon to surface.

"I'll need a raft and a man to row me ashore," said Remo. "My shoulders aren't up to rowing. Or swimming."

"Right. Will you need any help ashore?"

"I don't think so," said Remo. "I should be met."

"I rather doubt it," said Leahy. "We're way ahead of our estimated arrival time. You may have to wait ashore a long time for whoever it is is supposed to meet you."

"There'll be someone there," said Remo stubbornly, working one toe against the other heel, trying to get on his soft Italian leather slipons.

So Captain Lee Enright Leahy was not totally surprised when his submarine moved in close to the shore and he popped up the periscope and scanned the shoreline and saw, standing on the sand, looking out toward the *USS Darter,* the aged Oriental, wearing a bright red brocaded robe, pacing back and forth, obviously oblivious to the cold.

"Of course, he's here," Leahy mumbled to himself. "We left him here, he's been here ever since, and this other looneytoon is going to get off here and the two of them are going to wait and I'm going to come back twice more with two more people until they have a full table for bridge. The whole country's going nuts."

"Beg pardon, sir," said the executive officer.

"Surface and let's prepare to put our cargo ashore,"

said Leahy. "Before he decides to become a teapot."

"Aye, aye, sir," said the exec. Turning away, he mumbled "teapot, eh?" and decided that Captain Leahy would have to be watched.

CHAPTER TWELVE

"So this is it, huh?" said Remo as he limped through the shallow rock-bottomed water onto the shore. Behind him, the two sailors in the rubber raft used their oars to push the craft away from the shoreline and to hustle back to the waiting submarine.

Chiun stepped toward Remo, a smile lighting his face.

"Yes," he said. "This is it. The Pearl of the Orient." He waved his arms dramatically right and left. "The Sun Source of the World's Wisdom. Sinanju."

Remo's eyes followed Chiun's arms to the left and right. To the left was barren, rockstrewn desolation; to the right was more barren, rockstrewn desolation. The waves broke white, bubbling, and cold on the shore.

"What a dump," said Remo.

"Ah, but wait until you see the fishing building," said Chiun.

Using his cane for support, Remo hobbled forward again toward Chiun. Water squished from his soaked loafers but he did not feel the cold. Chiun's face squinted up as he seemed to see, for the first time, the cane in Remo's hand.

"Aiiieeee." His left hand flashed sideways, almost glinting in the brittle November sunlight of Sinanju. The broad leading edge of his hand hit the cane. The wood snapped and broke. Remo got his weight off it just quickly enough to avoid falling into the water. He stood there, holding the curved crook of the cane in his right hand, the rest of the cane bobbing in the water behind his back, before seeming to fight its way over the waves and back out toward the sea.

"Dammit, Chiun, I need that."

"I do not know what they have taught you in America while I was gone, but no disciple of the Master of Sinanju will use a walking stick. People will look. They will say, look, there is the disciple of the Master, and how young he is and he walks with a stick and how foolish of the Master to have tried to train such a pale piece of pig's ear to do anything. And they will scoff at me and I will not have it in my own land. What is wrong with you that you think you need a cane?"

"Three attacks, Little Father," Remo said. "Both shoulders and right leg."

Chiun searched Remo's face to determine if he knew the significance of the three attacks. The thin set of Remo's lips showed that he did.

"Well, we must go on to my palace," said Chiun, "and there we will care for you. Come."

He turned and walked away along the beach. Remo, using his left leg to move, and dragging his right leg heavily, hobbled after him. But he could not keep up, as Chiun widened the distance between them.

Finally, Chiun stopped ahead of Remo and gazed around him as if examining the majesty of his kingdom. Remo caught up to him. Without a word, Chiun turned and continued along the path he had taken, but this time more slowly, and Remo was able to stay at his side.

Fifty yards farther along, they stopped atop a small rise.

"There," said Chiun, pointing off in the distance. "The new fishing building."

Remo looked where Chiun pointed. A shanty of old water-logged planks and rolled tarpaper roofing perched precariously atop a deck that itself was perched delicately atop wooden pilings. It looked as if one sardine over the legal limit would topple it into the bay.

"What a dump," said Remo.

"Ahhh, to you it looks like a dump but it is highly efficient. The people of Sinanju have built it just right, to do its work. They are not interested in things for show, for the sake of show. Function is important. Come, I will show it to you. Would you like to see it?"

"Little Father," said Remo. "I would like to go to your house."

"Ah, yes. The American to the end. Not wishing to look and to learn from the wisdom of other people. It would not be right for you to try to learn how to build fishing buildings. That would make sense. Suppose someday you are without work? You could say, aha, but I can build fishing buildings and maybe that would keep you from standing on line for charity. But no, that requires foresight, of which you have none. And industry, of which you have less. No. Fritter your time away like the grasshopper, which finds itself in winter with nothing to eat."

"Chiun, please. Your house," said Remo, who stood only with great pain.

"It is all right," said Chiun. "I am used to your laziness. And it is a palace, not a house," and he turned left and began trudging along a sandy dirt road toward a small cluster of buildings several hundred yards away.

Remo hobbled to keep up with him.

"Didn't you once tell me, Little Father, that every time you entered the village, they threw flower petals in your path?" asked Remo, noticing that the road to the village center was empty of people and that Chiun, for all the so-called majesty of his office, might have been just another golden-ager out for a walk.

"I have suspended the flower petal requirement," said Chiun officiously.

"Why?"

"Because you are an American. I knew you might be misunderstanding of it. It is all right. The people protested but in the end I prevailed. I do not need flower petals to remind me of the love of my subjects."

No one met them on the street. No vehicles were to be seen. There were only a few stores and Remo could see people inside them but none came out to greet Chiun.

"You sure this is Sinanju?" asked Remo.

"Yes. Why do you ask?"

"Because it seems that a town you support and that your family has supported for centuries ought to pay a little more attention to you," said Remo.

"I have suspended the attention-paying requirement," said Chiun. His manner, Remo noticed, was less official and sounded a little like an apology. "Because . . ."

"I know, because I'm an American."

"Right," said Chiun. "But remember, even if they do not come out, people are watching. I wish you would walk right and not embarrass me by seeming to be an old man, old before your time, older even than your western dissolution would seem to require."

"I will try, Little Father, not to embarrass you," said Remo and, by an effort of will, he forced himself to put some weight on his injured right leg, reducing the limp, and, even though each motion pained him, he forced himself to swing his arms from the shoulders almost normally as he walked.

"There is the ancestral palace," said Chiun, motioning ahead with a nod of his head.

Remo looked ahead. Into his mind flashed a building he had once seen in California. It had been created by its builder from junk, made of broken bottles and tin cans and styrofoam cups and old tires and broken pieces of boards.

Chiun's house reminded Remo of a house built by the same craftsman, but this time with access to more materials, for in a village of wooden shanties and huts, Chiun's home was made of stone and . . .

And . . . glass and steel and wood and rock and shell. It was a low, one-story building whose architecture seemed to be American ranch as seen through an LSD haze.

"It's . . . it's . . . it's . . . really something to see," said Remo.

"It has been in my family for centuries," said Chiun. "Of course, I had it remodeled many years ago. I put in a bathroom which I thought was a good idea you westerners had. And a kitchen with a stove. See, Remo, I am willing to take advice when it is good."

Remo was pleased to hear that, for he had some additional good advice for Chiun—tear it down and start all over. He decided to tether his tongue.

Chiun led Remo to the front door, apparently made of wood. Only apparently, because the door had been totally covered over with shells of clams, oysters, and mussels. The door looked like a section of Belmar Beach four hours after a New Jersey rip tide.

The door was heavy and Chiun pushed it open with seeming difficulty. He looked at Remo almost apologetically.

"I know," said Remo. "You have suspended the door opening requirement."

"How did you know?"

"Because I'm an American," said Remo.

While Remo had considered the building's exterior as ugly, not even that had prepared him for the inside. Every available inch of floor space seemed to have something on it. There were jugs and vases and plates, there were statues and swords, there were masks and baskets, there were piles of cushions in place of chairs, there were low tables of highly-polished wood, there were colored stones in glass jars.

Chiun spun around and indicated his domain with another sweep of his hand.

"Well, Remo, what do you think?"

"I am underwhelmed," said Remo.

"I knew you would be," said Chiun. "These are all the prizes of the Masters of Sinanju. Tribute paid us by rulers from all over the world. From the Sun King as you call him. From Ptolemy. From the shahs of those countless countries that make grease. From the emperors of China when they remembered to pay their bills. From tribes of India. From a once-great nation of black Africa."

"Who ripped you off giving you a jar of colored stones?" asked Remo, looking at a jar which stood in the corner of the room, a foot and a half high, filled with dull stones.

"How American you are," said Chiun.

"Well, I mean one of your ancestors got hustled."

"The jar was the agreed-upon price."

"A jar filled with rocks?"

"A jar filled with uncut diamonds."

Remo looked at the jar again. It was true. It was filled with uncut diamonds and the smallest was two inches across.

"But I would not expect you to understand that," said Chiun. "For you, for the western mind, all the world is divided into two categories: shiny and not shiny. For you, a piece of glass. But for a Master of Sinanju, diamonds. Because we can look under the dullness and see the value of the core."

"Like you did with me?" said Remo.

"Even Masters of Sinanju sometimes get fooled. Something that is supposed to be an uncut diamond may turn out to be just a rock."

"Chiun, I wanted to ask you something."

"Ask me anything."

"I wanted to know," and then Remo felt the strength draining from his limbs and he knew that his muscles had been extended beyond the point that they

143

could be extended, and his right leg started to cave, and suddenly the effort of will ended, and his shoulders were blazing with pain. He opened his mouth to say something more, but he couldn't, and then he was falling toward the floor of the room.

He did not remember hitting the floor. He did not remember being lifted.

He only remembered waking up and looking around. He was in a small sunlit room, lying on a pile of cushions, naked, covered only with a thin silken sheet.

Chiun stood by his side and when Remo's eyes opened, he knelt. Carefully but quickly, his hands began to remove the bandages from Remo's shoulders.

"The doctor put those on," said Remo.

"The doctor is a fool. No muscle is helped by being strapped. Rest, yes. Inprisonment, no. We will make you well soon. We will . . ." but his voice trailed off as he saw Remo's right shoulder, as the last strand of bandage fell off.

"Oh, Remo," he said in a sad, pained voice. He said nothing further as he unwrapped the left shoulder and then he said it again, "Oh, Remo."

"The one who hit the leg was the best of all," Remo said. "Wait until you see it." He paused. "Chiun, how did you know I would come here?"

"What do you mean?"

"When you said goodbye to Smith, you said I would be here."

Chiun shrugged as he bent toward the bandage on Remo's right thigh. "It is written that you would."

"Written where?" asked Remo.

"On the men's room wall at Pittsburgh Airport,"

said Chiun nastily. "In the books of Sinanju," he said.

"And what does it say?" asked Remo.

Chiun deftly removed the bandage from Remo's thigh. This time he said nothing.

"That bad, huh?"

"I have seen worse," said Chiun. "Although not on anybody who survived."

He took a bowl from a small table near Remo's sleeping mat. "Drink this," he said. He lifted Remo's head and brought a cup to Remo's lips. The liquid was warm and almost tasteless except for what seemed to be a trace of salt.

"Awful. What is it?"

"It is a mixture from the seaweed that will start making you well again."

He let Remo's head down slowly. Remo felt tired. "Chiun," he said in a questioning voice.

"Yes, my son."

"You know who did this to me, don't you?"

"Yes, my son, I know."

"He is coming, Little Father," said Remo. His eyelids grew heavier as he spoke. It seemed as if his words were being spoken by someone else.

"I know, my son. He is coming."

"He may try to hurt you, Little Father."

"Sleep now, Remo. Sleep and heal."

Remo's eyes closed and he began to drift off. He heard Chiun's voice again. "Sleep and heal, my son."

And then Chiun's final words. "Heal quickly."

CHAPTER THIRTEEN

And thus it came to pass that the Master of Sinanju did walk along the path in the village where he had once been of such honor.

His feet were heavy, as was his heart, because he knew that powerless, unprotected was the young disciple from the land across the sea, and because he knew that the evil force that would destroy that disciple would soon make its appearance on the rocky soil of Sinanju.

And the Master thus had no patience with the tongues of fools, and when people approached him on the path, to talk about the young disciple, about the leadenness of his step, about the infirmities that seemed as if they were of age, the Master had no patience with them and flailed about and scattered them as the barking dogs scatters the goose. But he did not harm the people who gave him such aggravation, because it has always been written, since the dawn of writing, that the Master must not raise his hand in anger to harm a person from the village.

And it was this very command that gave the Master such pain of spirit. Because the one who was coming to destroy the young disciple was of the village of Sinanju, yea, even of the blood of the Master, and the Master could find no way in which he might violate his ages-old vow and inflict upon that one the death he deserved.

Yea, as the Master walked alone, he thought that his disciple, injured as he was, defenseless as a babe as he was, that his disciple would be killed, and Chiun, the Master of Sinanju, could not protect him because of his vow never to hurt someone from the village.

CHAPTER FOURTEEN

Premier Kim Il Sung was at the plain wooden desk in his office in the People's Building in Pyongyang when the secretary entered the room.

The secretary was a young captain of artillery. He affected a gabardine military uniform instead of the rough canvas-textured khaki that was official government issue, but Sung had never held this against him because he was a good secretary.

Communists could come and Communists could go; military styles could come and go; pride even could come and go, but good secretaries were to be nurtured.

Once, years before, Sung had been accused of turning into a reactionary rightwinger after seizing power, and he had explained in what he considered his gentle voice that all revolutionaries become conservatives after gaining power. "Radicalism is fine for revolution," he had said, "but conservatism is what gets the trucks out of the garage in the morning."

He had then displayed his continuing revolutionary zeal by throwing the insulter into a prison for two weeks. When the man was released, Sung summoned him to his office.

The man, a minor official from one of the provinces, had stood before Sung, humiliated, chastened.

"Now you know you cannot judge everything by appearances," Sung had said. "It was an easy lesson for you to learn because you are still alive. Many have not been so lucky."

So it was that Kim Il Sung rated his secretary by secretarial standards and not by any standard of appearance set for soldiers. And so it was that Sung rated the man his secretary ushered in to see him, not by his size or his clothing or his speech, but by a kind of internal fire that seemed to come through the man's eyes and that invested all his words with power.

"I am Nuihc," the man said, "and I have come to serve you."

"Why am I so lucky?" said Sung.

He saw immediately that the man named Nuihc had no sense of humor.

"Because it is through you that I can regain the hereditary title of my family. Master of Sinanju."

"Yes," said Kim Il Sung. "I have met the Master. He is a charming old rogue."

"He is a very old man," said Nuihc. "It is time for him to tend his vegetable garden."

"Why do you bother me with this?" asked Kim Il Sung. "Who cares what a small band of brigands does in one tiny village?"

He had chosen his words carefully and was rewarded by a small flash of anger in Nuihc's eyes.

"You know, my Premier, that that is not so," said Nuihc. "The House of Sinanju has for centuries been famed in the ruling palaces of the world. Now it is up to you to decide whether or not you wish the house to be run by a Westerner . . . an American. Because that is the choice. Who will be the new Master: Me? Or an American who represents the CIA and the other spy agencies of the government in Washington?"

"And again, I ask, why does it concern me?"

"You know the answer to that," said Nuihc. "First, our nation will be a laughing stock if this hereditary house becomes the property of an American. And second, the powers of the House are well known to you. Those powers could be put to use in your behalf, to the benefit of your rule. Not as they are now, working for the capitalists of Wall Street. Do you know, for a certainty, that the power of Sinanju will not be turned against you tomorrow or the next day? Whenever Washington wills it, Premier, you will pass into the pages of history for the dead, killed in office. You can prevent that."

Sung thought about those words for a long while before answering. He had met Chiun, and there had seemed to spring up almost a bond of friendship, but the old man had told him that he worked for the United States. This Nuihc might be right. One day, a word might come and soon Kim Il Sung would be dead.

On the other hand, what guarantee did Sung have that Nuihc would be any better? He looked carefully into Nuihc's face. His blood relationship with the old man was obvious; there were the same lines of face and body, the same feeling of coiled spring tension when the man only stood casually in front of Sung's desk.

"You wonder," Nuihc said, "whether or not you can trust me."

"Yes."

"You can trust me for one reason. I am driven by greed. The leadership of the House will give me power and wealth. Beyond that, I want our nation to rise high in the world; I want it to happen because at the side of Kim Il Sung is Nuihc, the new Master of Sinanju."

Kim Il Sung thought again for a long while, then he said, "I will consider it. In the meantime, you may avail yourself of the hospitality of my house."

It was almost dark when Chiun returned to his home. Remo still slept. The Korean girl who was Chiun's servant knelt by the white man's side, occasionally blotting up the sweat from his brow.

"Be gone," said Chiun.

The girl rose and bowed deferentially toward Chiun.

"He is very ill, Master."

"I know, child."

"He has no strength. Are white people always so weak?"

Chiun looked at her sharply but could tell she meant no disrespect. Yet here she was, Chiun's servant, the one loyal follower in the village, and even she could not hide her disappointment that Chiun had picked a white man to learn the role of the Master for that day when Chiun would rule no longer.

He struggled to keep his temper, then said softly, "Many are weak, child. But this one was strong, a giant among men, until he was brought down by the cunning attacks of a cowardly jackal's henchmen, a jackal too cowardly to attack himself."

"That is terrible, Master," said the girl, her face and voice ringing with the earnestness of someone who wanted desperately to believe. "I wish I could meet this jackal."

"You shall, child. You shall. And so shall he," Chiun said. He looked at Remo as if looking at a faraway cloud and then returned to the present moment and chased the girl from the room.

"Heal quickly, Remo," he said softly in the silent room. "Heal quickly."

Nuihc had not tried to leave the room that Kim Il Sung had provided for him in the palace. He was not worried by the guards he knew were outside the door, but he was waiting for an answer.

At dinner time, there was a knock on the door.

It opened before Nuihc could speak.

Kim Il Sung was there. He saw Nuihc sitting on a chair, looking out the window, toward the east, toward west, toward Sinanju. He smiled.

"Tomorrow we go to Sinanju," Sung said. "To crown a new master."

"You have chosen wisely," said Nuihc. He smiled also.

CHAPTER FIFTEEN

The caravan arrived in Sinanju shortly after noon the next day.

There was a lead car in which sat Kim Il Sung and Nuihc, followed by a car containing the governor of the province and Sung's adviser Myoch'ong. Lesser party officials followed in other cars, and while their mission was to drive the hated American influence from the history of Sinanju, none of them thought it incongruous that they drove in Cadillacs and Lincolns and Chryslers. The motorcycle escort of soldiers, six in front, six behind, six on each side, drove Hondas.

The caravan was spotted more than a mile outside the city, on the paved road leading to the town which had grown up around the old village of Sinanju. Within minutes, word had reached the old quarter that the premier was coming, along with the real Master of Sinanju, and in only moments word was at the home of Chiun.

"Master," said the granddaughter of the carpenter to Chiun, who sat on a mat staring through one of the house windows toward the bay, "many men are coming."

"Yes?"

"The premier is with them. And so, they say, is one of your blood."

Chiun turned slowly on the mat to look at the girl.

"Know one thing, child. When trouble comes, it

comes at its own time, never at yours. Even now, how quickly comes the day of darkness."

He turned back toward the sea and folded his arms and seemed to gaze beyond the bay, as if searching for a land where the sun might yet be shining.

"And what shall I do, Master?"

"Nothing. There is nothing we can do." Chiun's voice sounded old and tired.

The girl stood for a moment, waiting for more, then walked slowly away, confused and not really understanding why the Master was so deeply depressed.

The caravan of cars skirted the main city of Sinanju, turned toward the shoreline, then followed a dirty sand road that led into the heart of the old village.

They halted in the square in the center of town, and Nuihc and the premier stepped out onto the street. The premier wore his military tunic, Nuihc a two-piece black fighting costume. In the custom of Sinanju, it was unbelted. Fighting uniforms were belted for demonstrations; for fights to the death, no belts were worn. This tradition dated back four hundred years when two of Chiun's ancestors had fought for the vacant title of Master of Sinanju. One of the contenders wore a uniform with belt. Five minutes later he had been strangled with the belt. Since that time, no Master had worn a belted uniform except in exercise, practice, or demonstration. But never in combat.

Nuihc looked up and down the streets. He could see people peering through their windows but afraid to come out onto the street until they knew more about this caravan and its meaning.

"It has been many years since I walked this ground," said Nuihc. A heavy breeze blew off the bay and swirled his long, shiny black hair about his face. His eyes were narrowed into slits that looked like knife-cuts in smooth yellow flesh.

Kim Il Sung saw Nuihc's eyes and the blood lust in them, and it was there as if it always belonged there, and for just a moment Sung again wondered if it were not just a matter of time before that lust was turned upon him.

Chiun's palace was at the end of the street, thirty yards from the square, and now Nuihc looked at it and his face broke into a smile.

"Let us do it," he said.

Without waiting for an answer, he stepped off through the dust and sand toward the house of the Master of Sinanju. Kim Il Sung remained standing alongside his vehicle. Purposefully, conscious of the eyes watching him, Nuihc strode to the front door of Chiun's home and pounded on the door with his fist. Under the hammering, shells cracked and broke loose and powdered the wooden step in front of the door.

"Who is there?" answered a young woman's voice after a long pause.

"Nuihc is here," said the long-haired man in a loud ringing voice. "Descendant of the Masters of Sinanju, himself the new Master of Sinanju. Send out the American weakling and the senile traitor who has given him our secrets."

There was a long pause.

Then the woman's voice again.

"Go away. No one is home."

Nuihc pounded upon the door again. "There is no

hiding for you, old man, not for you or for the white lackey you would impose upon the people of this village. Come out of there before I come in and drag you out by the scruff of your scrawny neck."

Another pause.

The woman's voice again.

"It is not permitted to enter the Master's house without the Master's permission. Be gone, urchin."

Nuihc paused as it seeped into his head what Chiun's game was. Nuihc was protected in anything he said to Chiun because the old man, as Master of Sinanju, was not permitted to raise a hand against another from the village. But that protection ended should Nuihc enter Chiun's home uninvited, and Chiun could have the right to deal with him as just another burglar. Nuihc did not like the prospect. Still, how to get the old man and the American out of the house?

He walked back, jauntily, toward Kim Il Sung. His mind was clicking and he knew the answer.

He spoke to the premier, and then Sung and his entourage followed Nuihc back to the house.

Again Nuihc pounded on the door. Again the woman answered: "Go away, I told you."

"The premier is here," said Nuihc, raising his voice to be sure both Chiun and the villagers heard.

There was a pause.

The woman's voice again.

"Tell him he is in the wrong place. The nearest brothel is in Pyongyang."

Nuihc spoke out crisply. "Tell the old man that unless he and the imperialist white swine come out, the premier will order this house destroyed by explosion

156

for being what it is: a spy's den giving comfort to an enemy of the state." He turned and smiled at Sung.

Another pause. Longer this time.

Finally the woman's voice again: "Return to the village square. The Master will meet you there."

"Tell him to hurry," ordered Nuihc. "We do not have time to waste on the doddering of the ancient." He turned and walked alongside the premier, back the thirty yards to the village square, where they waited by the premier's Cadillac. Now they were not alone. The people of Sinanju, who had been watching and listening from inside their homes and shops, now stepped out onto the old wooden sidewalks and, as the premier and Nuihc passed, they cheered.

Inside his home, Chiun had heard Nuihc's final ultimatum and now he heard the cheers and knew what they were for. He stared out toward the bay. After all these years, after all his service, after all the centuries of tradition, it had come to this: a Master of Sinanju, humiliated in his own village by one of his own family, with the village citizens cheering the intruder.

How pleasant it would be to do what should be done. To step out into the square and to reduce Nuihc to the pile of flesh and bone chip that he should be. But the centuries of tradition that had given him pride also gave Chiun responsibility. He was disgraced now before the villagers, but he would be disgraced in his own eyes if he should strike Nuihc.

The younger man knew that, and the knowledge of his freedom from attack had emboldened his tongue.

It should have been Remo, Chiun knew. It was for Remo to meet this challenge, to destroy Nuihc for once and all. So it had been written in the books ages

157

before. But Remo lay asleep, his muscles unable to work, more helpless than a child.

And because neither Remo nor Chiun could raise an arm against Nuihc, the title of Master of Sinanju was going to pass, for the first time in unremembered centuries, into the hands of one who would not wear it with pride and honor.

Chiun rose from his mat and went into the main living section of the house and he lit a candle. From a chest, he took a long white robe, the robe of innocence, and a black fighting uniform. He fingered the black uniform fondly, then dropped it atop the chest. He would wear the white robe, the color of the unspoiled. The color of the chicken.

He donned the robe quickly then kneeled before the candle and prayed to his ancestors. In that moment was crystallized all the training of Sinanju, because its root was: to survive.

And Chiun had made his decision. He would give up the title of Master. He would trade it for Remo's life. And then one day, when Remo was well, there might be a chance for Remo to reclaim that title.

It would do Chiun no good. He would, by that time, have been marked in history as a disgrace, the first Master ever forced to give up his title. But at least the title might one day be wrested from Nuihc, and that was some small measure of consolation.

Chiun reached forward a delicate long-nailed finger and extinguished the candle flame by squeezing the wick between thumb and index finger. He rose to his feet in one fluid movement that left his robe still and unswirling.

"Master?" said the girl, appearing next to him.

158

"Yes?" said Chiun.

"Must you go?"

"I am the Master. I cannot run."

"But they do not want you. They want the American. Give him up."

"I am sorry, child," said Chiun. "But he is my son."

The woman shook her head. "He is white, Master."

"And he is more my son than any yellow man. He shares not my blood but he shares my heart and my mind and my soul. I cannot give him up." And Chiun touched the girl lightly on her cheek and walked toward the front door.

In the square, the villagers crowded near the car where Nuihc and the premier stood. The motorcycle soldiers kept them at a respectful distance, but their voices spoke out clearly.

"The Master is too old."

"He betrayed us by giving the secrets to the white man."

"Nuihc will restore the honor of Sinanju."

Some felt they should say that Chiun's labors had always supported the village, that it was not given to mere villagers to know what was on the Master's mind, and that the poor did not starve and the elderly were not discarded and the babies were not drowned, sent home to the sea, anymore because of Chiun's efforts. But they did not say these things because it seemed no one wished to hear them, and instead all wished to heap praise upon Nuihc who preened himself and soaked up the adulation as he stood by the premier.

"Where is he?" asked Kim Il Sung of Nuihc.

His answer did not come from Nuihc. The crowd was silent, its humming babble stopped in midword. All eyes turned toward Chiun's home.

Coming down the street slowly, down the thirty yards toward the cars and the crowd and his tormentor, came Chiun, his face impassive, his steps slow but light, his hands folded within each other inside the voluminous sleeves of his traditional white robe.

"Where is the American?" one man called.

"The false Master still protects the westerner," said another in outrage.

"Traitor," screamed another man.

And then the voices rose above the tiny square, "Traitor! Traitor! Traitor!"

Back inside Chiun's house, the young woman who was his servant heard the catcalls and the hoots and her eyes watered with tears. How could they? How did they dare to do such a thing to the Master? And finally she realized the reason. It was not the Master they hated, but the white American. For the white American, the Master was doing this.

It was not fair. The Master's life destroyed because of the American.

The American would not escape the responsibility for his being. She went to the living room and from a pearl-encrusted scabbard withdrew a highly polished knife with a long, curved blade.

Holding it behind her, she went into the room where Remo slept. His eyes were still closed. She knelt down beside the sleeping mat. She raised her eyes to the heavens and offered up a prayer to her ancestors, to understand what she was doing.

She looked down on the hated white man. "Lift the

160

knife up and drive it into his heart," a small voice whispered insistently inside her.

The white man's eyes opened. He smiled at her.

"Hi, sweetheart, where's Chiun?" he said.

She lifted the knife up over her head and willed herself to drive it down into Remo's chest, but then she let it drop from her hands and buried her face against Remo's chest, weeping.

CHAPTER SIXTEEN

"Where is the swine American?" Nuihc's voice was a sneer as he looked across the two feet of space separating him from Chiun.

Chiun ignored him. To the premier, he said: "I see you have chosen a side."

The premier shrugged.

"How like a creature from Pyongyang," said Chiun. "To cast his lot with a trollop."

One of the motorcycle soldiers stepped forward. He raised his pistol over his head to club Chiun for his insult. Chiun did not move. The pistol poised and Kim Il Sung barked: "Cease."

The soldier let his hand down slowly, then with a look of hatred at Chiun he backed away.

"Do not be angry," said Chiun. "Your premier has saved you to die another day."

"Enough," said Nuihc. "Remo. Where is he?"

"He rests," said Chiun.

"I have challenged him. He is a coward not to be here."

"A coward. A coward. The traitor has given the wisdom to a coward," came cries from the crowd.

Chiun waited until the noise subsided.

"Who is the coward?" said Chiun. "Is it the injured white man? Or is it the cowardly squirrel who used three people to have him injured?"

"Enough, old man," said Nuihc.

"Not enough," said Chiun. "You fool these people now into thinking how brave Nuihc is. Did you tell them how you last faced the American? In the museum of the whale? And how he left you tied up, with your own belt, like a child?"

Nuihc's face flushed. "He had help. He did not do it alone."

"And did you tell them how you tried to kill the Master, in the oil fields of that faraway land? And how I left you to dry in the sun like a starfish?"

"You talk much, old man," said Nuihc bitterly. "But I have come here to get rid of the American for good. And then I, not you, am the Master of Sinanju. Because you have betrayed your people by giving the secrets to a white man."

"Traitor!"

"Traitor!" came the voices again.

"You have forgotten the legend of the night tiger," said Chiun. "Of the dead man whose face is pale and who will come from the dead and be trained by the Master to be the night tiger who cannot die. You have forgotten these things."

"Your legends are for children," said Nuihc with a sneer. "Bring on your American and we will see who cannot die."

"Where is he?"

"The white man . . . bring him forward!"

The voices raised in a roar and under them, Chiun spoke softly to Nuihc. "You may have Sinanju, Nuihc. Let Remo live. That is my price."

Loudly, so he could be heard by all, Nuihc answered. "I do not deal with the senile and the foolish. Remo must die. And you must be sent home." A hush

163

fell over the crowd. In the old days, before the labors of the Masters of Sinanju had given the villagers sustenance, the old and the weak and the hungry babies were sent home—by being put into the cold waters of the bay to drown.

Chiun looked carefully into Nuihc's eyes. There was no mercy there, no pity, no flicker of humanity.

His final offer.

"I will send myself home," said Chiun. "But the man with white skin must live."

His voice was a tired plea for mercy for Remo.

His answer was a smile from Nuihc who said, "So long as he lives, Sinanju's secrets are not secrets. He has learned the ancient ways, now they must die with him. Now."

"Now!" came the cries.

"The American must die!"

And then it was that a voice rang over the shouts of the maddened townspeople. And so it was that they turned and cast their eyes toward the palace of the Master and a hush fell over them as there they saw, standing in the dust of the road, the white man dressed in a two-piece black suit without belt.

And his voice rang over the heads of the villagers like an alarm bell and they looked at each other in amazement because the white man spoke in the tongue of the villagers, and his words were the words of that land and its old ways, and what he did say was.

"I am created Shiva, the Destroyer, death the shatterer of worlds. The dead night tiger made whole by

164

the Master of Sinanju. What is this dog meat that now challenges me?"

And the crowd was hushed, for their tongues were coated with the powder of fear.

Chiun was looking at Nuihc when Remo's voice sounded. The old man saw Nuihc's eyes widen with surprise and perhaps fear.

Kim Il Sung looked shocked, also frightened, but fright could be forgiven in one who was not of the House of Sinanju.

Chiun turned slowly. Had the gods heard his prayers and visited a miracle of healing upon Remo?

But the hope faded when he saw Remo, standing there heavily, most of his weight on his uninjured left leg, his hands and arms still hanging awkwardly close to his body, resting on his hip bones to take the pressure of their weight off his damaged shoulders.

When Chiun thought of the pain Remo had endured to dress and to walk down that dusty road to the village square, his heart filled with love, but also pity because now Remo faced Nuihc's murderous vengeance.

Nuihc saw too. He saw the wrists resting awkwardly on hips; he saw the weight resting heavily on Remo's left leg. With a smile that promised death, he walked from the small group of men toward Remo.

Remo stood there, his brain throbbing from the pain of his walk. Nuihc was supposed to deliver the fourth blow to Remo's left leg, the blow that would cripple or kill him.

He had a chance if Nuihc got careless. If he got

close enough to Remo, the bigger American might be able to drag him down with his weight and get in some kind of blow. It was all he had. As he looked up and saw Nuihc's eyes meeting his, he knew it would not be enough.

Over Nuihc's head, Remo could see Chiun standing still, his face draped in sorrow. He knew the torment that must be in Chiun's mind now—his affection for Remo, and his refusal to disgrace the House by hitting a villager, even if that villager was Nuihc.

Nuihc stopped now. He was out of Remo's reach.

"So you still walk," he said.

"Get on with it, dog meat," said Remo.

"As you will."

Remo waited for him to come closer, to deliver the fourth stroke, the one to Remo's left leg.

Nuihc did not do it. His right leg flashed out and the point of his foot smashed into the knot of muscles at Remo's right shoulder. Remo screamed as the muscles reseparated.

His wrist dropped from its resting place on his hip. The weight of his arm could not pain any more than the shoulder itself did.

Slowly Nuihc moved around behind Remo, as if the American were a stationary object. Remo could not turn to see the blow coming. He felt it land, inside the muscles in the back of his left shoulder. Again he screamed with the pain, as he could feel the fibers of muscle tearing.

Still he stood.

Nuihc was back in front of him, his face contorted with hatred.

"So you are Shiva?" he said. "You are a weak

166

white man, weak as all white men are weak, corrupted as all Americans are corrupted. How does this feel, night tiger?" he shouted and drove his left foot into the bunch of muscles in Remo's already injured right thigh.

Another scream.

Remo went down. His face hit into the dust. The powder coated his lips. His mind felt each muscle of his body and each one shouted its pain. He did not try to rise. He knew the effort was hopeless.

Nuihc stood over him. "I do not even need the fourth blow for you," he sneered. "I will save it for a few moments. Remember. It is coming."

He turned back to Chiun and Kim Il Sung.

The crowd cheered.

"Hail Nuihc. Hail the new Master. Look at the weak American." And they laughed as they pointed at Remo.

Nuihc walked away. Remo lay in the street, the dust on his lips, and he felt the dirt sticking to his face, and for a moment he did not know why it was sticking, and then he realized it was because he was crying.

And then even crying was too painful for him and he just lay in the street, hoping that Nuihc would kill him quickly.

Nuihc stood next to Chiun and Sung.

"There he is, eating the dirt of Sinanju. This is the one, the outsider to whom the ancient one gave the secrets because he said the white man was strong and wise. Look at him. Do you think him strong now?"

The townspeople looked again at Remo. One laughed aloud. And then another, and another, until

167

all of them were laughing as they looked at Remo, face down in the dirt, not moving.

Nuihc joined in the laughter and when they stopped, he asked in a loud voice, "And what do you think of the wisdom of one who picked that white man for his strength? I say, Chiun is too old. Too old to be your protector. Too old to be the Master of Sinanju. Too old for anything except to go home again as the aged and the weak and the foolish did in the olden times."

And the crowd lifted its voices.

"Go home, Chiun. Nuihc is our new Master. Send the ancient one home."

And in the dust, Remo heard the words and knew what they meant, and he wanted to cry out, "Chiun, save yourself, these people aren't worth your spit," but he couldn't say it because he could not talk.

Remo heard the voices and then he heard another voice, a voice he had known for so many years, a voice that had brought him wisdom and had taught him at every step, but now it was a different voice, because all at once it seemed old and tired, and the voice said, "All right. I will go home."

It was Chiun but it didn't sound like Chiun's voice anymore. Chiun's real voice was different. It was strong. Once when he had been dying of burns, Remo had heard Chiun's voice and it had been strong in his head and it had said, "Remo, I will not let you die. I am going to make you hurt, Remo, but you will live because you are supposed to live."

And another time when Remo had been poisoned, through the mists he had heard the voice of Chiun, saying: "Live, Remo, live. That is all I teach you, to

168

live. You cannot die, you cannot grow weak, you cannot grow old unless your mind lets you do it. Your mind is greater than all your strength, more powerful than all your muscles. Listen to your mind, Remo, it is saying to you: live."

That was Chiun's voice, and this old man's voice that had said it was going to allow itself to die, that wasn't Chiun's voice, Remo told himself. It was an impostor's voice, because Chiun would not die and Remo would tell him that. Remo would tell him, Chiun, you must live. But to tell him that he had to be able to move.

His right arm was flung out in front of him. He forced himself, through the pain, to feel the dust under his fingertips. He moved his index finger. He felt the dust and dirt slide up under his fingernail. Yes, Chiun, see, I am alive, he thought, and I am alive because my mind says live, and I remember it, even if you don't, and then Remo made his right middle finger move.

His left hand was under his head. The pain burned his shoulder like a white-hot poker as he turned his hand a fraction of an inch under his head. But didn't you always tell me, Chiun, that pain is the price one pays to stay alive. Pain belongs to the living. Only the dead never hurt.

He could hear their voices again, Nuihc's loud and triumphant, demanding no delay, demanding that Chiun march now down to the sea and out into the bay until the waters covered him and he went home to his ancestors. And he heard Chiun's voice, soft and sad and weak, the voice of a man who has suffered a great loss, and he was saying he could not go home until he had made his peace with his ancestors.

Remo felt the knot of muscles in his right thigh and he could feel the separate tears in them, the tear that had first been opened by Lynette Bardwell and then reopened by Nuihc who had, in delivering the blow, done some new damage of his own.

Remo screwed his eyes tightly closed. He could feel the muscles, sense their existence, and pressing his lips together so he did not scream, he tensed the muscles and the pain was worse than any pain he had ever felt, but that's it, Chiun, isn't it, pain tells you you're alive.

He heard another voice now, it must have been from the Korean official who stood with Chiun and Nuihc because Remo did not recognize it. The voice said that Chiun could have a few minutes before he would go home and the American would be dispatched any way Nuihc decided, but his body would be sent to the American embassy as a protest against spies infiltrating the glorious People's Democratic Republic of North Korea.

His left leg still worked, Remo found, flexing the muscles from thigh to calf. And the most important muscle of all worked. His mind. His mind was the master of the muscles, the intellect the ruler of the flesh, and he let them talk, he let them babble on, and he knew what he would do. He licked his lips to get the dust off them and he tasted the dirt on his tongue and it made him angry at himself for failing, angry at Chiun for surrendering, angry at Nuihc for always coming at them.

But mostly angry at himself.

He heard the voices talk on but he was not listening any more, he was speaking himself, speaking without

170

sound, but speaking in his mind to his muscles and they were hearing him because they moved.

The crowd stilled, and there was a tiny babble of voices, and over them came Nuihc's voice issuing his final ultimatum to Chiun: "You have five minutes, old man."

And then there was another voice Remo heard and he was surprised because it was his voice. He heard it say, loudly, as if he was not even in pain, and he thanked the mind for making the body work, and the voice said:

"Not yet, dog meat."

And there was a scream from the villagers as they all turned and saw Remo standing again. His black uniform was coated with the dust of the street, but he was standing, and the villagers could not believe it, but he was standing, staring at Nuihc and he was smiling.

When Nuihc turned again to face Remo, he could not disguise the look on his face, a look of shock and terror.

He stood there, death-still, alongside Chiun and the premier. Remo, hurting in every muscle, in every tendon and fiber and sinew, made the only move he had left.

He charged.

Perhaps surprise or shock might stop Nuihc from moving fast enough, and while Remo could not walk to him, his charge might get him to Nuihc before Remo fell down again. And if he could fall with Nuihc under him, then perhaps. Just perhaps.

Remo was lunging forward now, his body moving

lower and lower toward the earth, only the will of his forward motion preventing him from falling onto his face.

Three yards to go.

But Nuihc was in control again. He stood his ground ready to deal the final blow to Remo, and Remo saw it. When he was only a yard away, he let his body flip out to the right, and as he fell onto his damaged right shoulder he used all the power that was left in his body and concentrated it on his undamaged left leg and drove his bare left foot into the solar plexus of Nuihc. He felt the toe go in, deep, but he did not feel the crunch of bone, and he knew he had missed the sternum, he had hurt Nuihc but the blow was not fatal, and that was all Remo had left. As Remo lay on the ground, he looked up toward Chiun, in supplication, as if asking for forgiveness, and then he heard a scream and Nuihc's eyes bulged forward and he reached down with his hands to grasp his abdomen, but his hands never got there because Nuihc was pitching forward onto the ground.

He hit open mouth first and lay there, in a kneeling position, his eyes open, staring in death at the dirt of the street, as if it were the thing that interested him most in life and in death.

Remo looked at him carefully and realized that Nuihc was dead, and he did not know why, and he passed out because he didn't care.

Unconscious, Remo did not hear Chiun proclaim that Remo's courage was worth more than all Nuihc's skill and that Nuihc had not died of the blow but had died of fear and that now the villagers would know that the Master had selected wisely in choosing Remo.

And Remo did not hear the villagers proclaim undying allegiance to Chiun, and praise Remo for having the heart of a Korean lion in a white man's skin.

He did not hear the villagers drag off the body of Nuihc to cast it into the bay to feed the crabs, and he did not hear Chiun order the premier to have his soldiers carry Remo gently back to Chiun's palace, and he did not heard the premier promise that he would never again involve himself in Sinanju's internal matters, and that there would be an immediate end to the graft visited upon the tribute by the thieving governor.

Remo woke for just a fraction of an instant as he was being lifted by the soldiers, and in that fraction of an instant he heard Chiun's voice, strong again and demanding, order "gently," and before his eyes closed again, he saw that the fingernail of Chiun's left index finger was stained red.

Blood red.

And it was wet.

CHAPTER SEVENTEEN

When Remo opened his eyes again, it seemed as if the entire village of Sinanju had crowded into his bedroom to look at him.

Standing alongside him was Chiun, who was busy pointing out to the villagers that they should not be fooled. "He only looks American. Inside the best white man is a Korean trying to get out."

Remo looked around the room at the flat-faced villagers, who only a little while before had been ready to hand up not only Remo, but also Chiun, who had supported them for untold years, and he said: "I have something to say to all of you."

He looked around the room as Chiun translated his English words. He could see their attention grow stronger.

"I am an American," said Remo.

Chiun said something in Korean.

"I am proud of it, proud to be an American," Remo continued.

Chiun rattled off a string of Korean words.

"The next time you start talking about the weak Americans, perhaps you should think that it was an American who overcame the pain, a white American."

Chiun said something.

"And it was Nuihc, not only a Korean, but of your village, who was cowardly and died."

Chiun said something more.

"And I think his fate is what all of you deserve because as far as I'm concerned, you are a pack of back-biting worthless ingrates who all ought to be sent home to feed the fishes. If the fishes would have you."

Chiun said something and the villagers' faces broke into broad smiles and they applauded. Then Chiun ushered them out of the room and was alone with Remo.

"I think it lost something in the translation," said Remo.

"I delivered to them your coarse words," said Chiun. "Of course, I had to make minor changes to fit the idiom."

"Give me an example of a minor change," said Remo.

"I had to tell them so that they would understand, you see, that you had shown Korean heart, and that Nuihc had been softened by reactionary imperialism and that I would not have picked anyone weak to be my son, even if he was white, and . . . well, and so forth. It is not necessary to go on because it was all just as you said to say it."

There was a knock on the door and when Chiun opened it, Premier Kim Il Sung stood there.

"You are awake," he said to Remo in pleasantly flavored English.

"Yes. I am glad you speak English," said Remo.

"Why?" asked the premier.

"Because I have several things to say to you that I don't want Chiun to have to translate."

"He is very tired," interjected Chiun. "Perhaps some other time."

175

"Now will be fine," interrupted Remo. "Pyongyang is a whore city," he started off.

"Don't we know it," said Sung. "If you want to see a good town, you should come to Hamhung, my home town. That's a real place."

"If the people there are like the people here," said Remo, "you can stuff them."

"People are people everywhere," said Sung. "Even here. Even in America, I suppose."

Chiun nodded. Remo found it maddening not to be able to insult Sung.

"I was in Vietnam," Remo finally said. "I wasted a lot of Vietnamese!"

"Not enough," said Sung. "Vietnamese are like bird droppings. As far as I'm concerned, Hanoi is no better than Saigon. I sometimes wonder how the bird droppings tell themselves apart."

"I'd like to wipe out the whole Communist cong," said Remo.

Kim Il Sung shrugged. "It might not be a bad idea. Vietnam is the only country I ever heard of where the population increased during a war. I hope you didn't get too close to any Vietnamese. They're all diseased, you know."

"Oh, shit," Remo said and gave up. He turned his head away and looked out the window at the cold white Korean sky.

"I will leave," he heard Kim Il Sung say.

"You will arrange that the tribute is no longer stolen by your thieving ministers here," said Chiun.

"I will. The tribute now comes under my protection."

Chiun nodded. He escorted Sung to the door and as

176

the premier left, said to him in a stage whisper: "Don't be upset by anything he said. He's really a Korean at heart."

"I know," said Kim Il Sung.

Chiun closed the door and again was alone with Remo.

"Well?" said Remo.

"What well?"

"I'm sure you've got something to say. Say it."

"I am glad you brought it up, Remo. Your stroke against Nuihc was faulty. It was an inch too low to do any real good. In the old days, I would forgive such sloppiness because your improper American attitudes always make you sloppy. But now I can no longer excuse it. As soon as you are well, you must practice. Fortunately the villagers knew you were injured so they would excuse your sloppiness. You did not disgrace the House, but we must be sure you never do that again."

"Is that all you've got to say?"

"What else?"

"Why was your fingernail red?" asked Remo.

"My fingernail?"

"Yes. Your fingernail on your index finger of your left hand."

"In your delirium, you must have imagined it," said Chiun.

"You zapped Nuihc, didn't you?"

"Remo. What a terrible thing to say. You know that the Master is bound never to strike someone from the village. And I am the Master. Oh, maybe for a few seconds there, when Nuihc claimed to be the Master, maybe I was not the Master, but . . ."

"Don't give me any of that," interrupted Remo. "You were the Master and are the Master and if you zapped him, you shouldn't have."

"If I have done anything wrong, I will answer to my ancestors. But that is all yesterday and today. Now we must speak of tomorrow. Of the day when you, Remo, will become the Master of Sinanju."

Chiun threw his arms open wide, to encompass the entire bedroom with its assortments of pots and jars and vases.

"Just think, Remo, someday this will all be yours."

"Bring back Nuihc," Remo said, and for the first time in days, it didn't hurt to laugh.